Chosen: Book One

The Beautiful Side of Truth

By Kathryn Tracy

Chosen

Acknowledgements

To my friends, family, and all those who have supported me: I thank you very much and hope this book takes you away from your troubles into a new world. I love you all.

Chosen

Observing the love that binds people together is to have witnessed a powerful thing on Earth.

-Tiernay Bookless

Chapter 1

    In the midway between sleep and consciousness it was like something in my brain had clicked. Suddenly I was wide-awake. The hairs on the back of my neck stood on end, *something was wrong*. I threw the sheets off me and toppled onto the floor landing on my feet causing a thud. It was the middle of the night and I couldn't see a thing. My eyes had not yet adjusted to the darkness. Slowly I stood from my crouching position, feeling my way towards the door. I fumbled for the handle of my bedroom door, flung the door open and rounding a bend flew down the hallway towards the front door, my exit, my escape. I anxiously awaited my freedom and the feeling of fresh air reaching my lungs. Sweat began to bead on my forehead, not from my flight to the door but from nerves. As I neared the front door I got *that* feeling, the feeling that creeps into the pit of your stomach on those dark lonely nights telling you something is not right.

    And then it happened. Instantly I was surrounded. I counted five but it was hard to tell. Panicked, I made one last lunge for the front door but when I opened it I found myself face to face with another intruder. I stumbled backwards in shock. By now the five I had counted earlier had come out of the shadows and were closing in on me apparently I had counted right, so far there were only five of them minus the dude at the door. I could see them all clearly now from the moonlight streaming in through a window, a window I just now noticed was broken. There was a full moon out tonight. It took me a second before I realized I recognized one of them; the intruder in the doorway.

    "Rico?" I questioned accusingly. Ignoring me he stepped inside and made himself at home.

    "What are you doing here Rico," I said menacingly.

Chosen

He then threw himself on the couch, taunting me. "Love the outfit. Really, you dress up just for us?" he sneered.

Rico and I used to go the same middle school before he got kicked out. He was short for a guy with black hair and dark skin. He wore baggy jeans and a ghetto shirt with a naked woman on it.

I kept my mouth shut but he wanted me to go off on him, wanted to get a rise out me, and if he thought I was going to play into his hand he was wrong; I knew how guys like him worked. It was two a.m and I was in my pj's. My hair was sticking up at all ends, I wore an overlarge T-shirt that hung to my knees, and sleep shorts. I was barefoot down to my last pinky toe; no giant funky pink bunny slippers for me. I suddenly felt very exposed standing there in just my T-shirt and shorts.

I crossed my arms over my chest, "What do you want Rico?" I repeated demanding to know what he was doing here.

He stood, I started to take a step back but stopped, I would stand my ground. I wasn't afraid of him. This was still my house.

"No, I mean it," he cocked his head as if pondering something "Mickey, how *cute,*" he said indicating the insignia of the Mickey Mouse caricature displayed on my t-shirt, letting his fingers play over the edge of my sleeve.

I slapped his hand away hard enough that it made a sound. It surprised him. I continued to glare at him. At that he threw his head back and let out a laugh that sounded more like the squawking of a dying chicken. I was very aware of the people at my back however; I was moreover so focused on Rico. I had to admit they had me cornered. The only thing I could hope for is they get on with what they came here for. I knew this wasn't the best idea but I was tired of feeling like a sitting duck.

"Hey Rico are you all talk and no walk?" This got his attention.

Chosen

He got right up in my face, "what's that?"

"You heard me, what are you doing here besides to take up space on my couch?"

That got him, anger flashed across his face for a split second and then he was Rico again.

"Well amigos looks like the chica here would prefer we get down to business," he said grinning.

This time when he stepped towards me I stepped back for when he looked at me only one word came to mind, "prey". He turned away from me, and then caught me by surprise as he slapped me so hard I fell to the floor. I tried to get back up and was halfway there but he shoved me back down. I struggled but froze when he pulled out a switchblade. I swallowed the gasp that had formed in my throat as my eyes followed the switchblade closely. He held it to my throat. The thought of that cold steel against my skin never left my thoughts for a second. Rico was grinning at me, watching me squirm. I stared straight into his eyes giving him the coldest stare I could muster. The smell of cigarette smoke smothered me, made me want to gag, Rico reeked of the junk. He pushed the blade threateningly closer to my neck.

"We have a message for you little chica," he said. Then he leaned in closer positioning his mouth directly beside my ear. Whispering in my ear he said each word slowly and with precision. "You ...*ever*... come... near... the... Snakes... territory... again, I'll kill you".

My eyes widened. The Snakes were a street gang. Commonly known gang members had snake tattoos to mark their membership. I glanced down at Rico's forearm and there it was, the Snake tattoo. I had noticed it earlier, but thought nothing of it. Rico was part of a gang, when had this happened? This must be some part of his initiation to prove his *loyalty*. Rico then let the blade fall away. He stood. I wanted to get up however, I waited

Chosen

for them to leave, not moving; hardly breathing I watched them walk out the door one by one. When they were gone I let out a huge breath of air that I hadn't realized I'd been holding, relief washing over me. I stood, happy to be upright again. I went to the front door and very decidedly locked it as if that would keep all the bad guys away.

"First things first," I said thinking out loud "I have to get cleaned up." I needed to wash the stench of those creeps off me, and headed toward the bathroom.

Chapter 2

Early the next morning I was startled from a restless sleep by the sound of banging. It instantly made me jump. After regaining my senses I realized it must be my dad and older brother Tim.

"Emma, open the door! I can't find the spare key," called my dad from the other side of the door.

The clock on my bedside table displayed 9:00 a.m. It was a Sunday. I had tried to get some sleep after last night's events but to no avail. I rushed toward the banging to let in my dad and Tim. I looked through the peep hole first to make sure it was them. My dad and Tim must have just gotten back from his girlfriend's house. That's where the rest of my brothers were. We were in the process of moving. I had stayed behind to help get things organized and ready to move, at least I was supposed to when I must have fallen asleep and then those creeps showed up.

"Hey Emma, sorry I must have left the house key at Tarrasa's. Did we wake you? How'd you sleep?" asked dad, these questions flying past me as they walked in the door.

I decided to go for truth; because I had a feeling I looked it.

"No, you didn't wake me, I didn't sleep too well."

"Oh, well I'm sorry to hear that, Hun, how 'bout I make you some eggs while you get dressed?" Dad said helpfully.

"Yeah that would be great." I answered with a smile, suddenly realizing I was starving.

He had already pulled out a pan for the eggs when he asked me, "Did you finish packing up the rest of your boxes?"

"Yes," I lied, already on my way down the hall.

Chosen

"Dad?" I asked, once done getting dressed. "I was wondering, since I'm already packed if you guys could head on over to Tarrasa's house and I could meet you back there later." I proposed.

Dad, known to others as Phil, was a fairly tall man in his forties. He had fluffy brown hair, peppered gray; revealing his age. It was obvious that his hair and beard needed a trim, but other than that he was a pretty decent looking guy. Phil had known for some time now I was not happy with this move and he was not sure I was ok with Tarrasa either. Therefore Phil, seeing that I was in no mood to help with moving and figuring this to be the reason behind it, granted me permission to skip out on today. Good for him for if he hadn't I had a feeling he would have lost me forever. For at the moment I just really needed some space and was in no mood to deal with my family and Dad's new girlfriend.

Finishing my eggs I told my dad and Tim that I would meet them later and headed out the door. Outside I found that the streets were wet from last night's rain, the smell of which still lingered in the air. The sky was gray and just as the thought of more rain appeared in my head it began to sprinkle. Not wanting to get my hair wet I threw my hood over my head and headed out into the spray.

Chosen

Chapter 3

It being a Sunday afternoon there was no school. However Carmen Jockolva had the unfortunate task of participating in a meeting for her mother. Her mother, Catherine Jockolva, was a large business owner who inherited the business from her father. Although she herself was not much of a business woman she intended to make Carmen one, hence the meeting. The meeting had just started and she had already started twisting back and forth in a rolling office chair. After a few irritated glances from the members of the board she stopped. The wide glass windows let in little light due to blinds to cut the sun's glare on particularly bright days. There was no need for them today. The room was small just enough room for a table and some people, meeting size she guessed. Carmen wasn't much of the corporate type, never was and never would be. She was just itching to get out of her white blouse, grey blazer and matching skirt and into regular clothes. Not to mention her heels were killing her. Until then however, she would just have to sit through this meeting listening to this person drone on and on; who knows how long she'd last.

The rain had begun to die down. Walking across the building's parking structure I found myself face to face with Jockolva Industries. Its' double doors were shiny and waiting. Pulling on the gold handle I walked into the company lobby and approached one of the elevators. The elevator music was tacky as usual, they should probably update those I was thinking to myself, of course then it might not be elevator music. Once on the fourth floor I was greeted by the bustle of people busy at work. At least that's what you would *think* you would see in a Corporate Industry right? No, the first thing I was greeted with was at least ten people standing around a water cooler. However, I had only just walked a few steps when an employee rounding a corner too fast knocked me over, carrying a stack of files and a coffee mug which he preceded to spill all over himself and me. The clumsy fool in question was dressed in business attire and looked to be about in his early twenties, probably an intern.

After a few minutes of fussing over his coffee stain he helped me to my feet, "If you're trying to get first in line for the water cooler you're a little late." I retorted.

"I'm sorry I didn't see you there, I was just delivering these files to accounting," he says as he starts to gather up the scattered files.

"My name's Burt by the way."

The name Burt could be seen clearly displayed on his name tag.

"Emma," I reply, introducing myself, "Emma Carter."

"Well, Emma is there anything I can help you with?"

"Yes, actually I'm looking for a friend, I'm told she is in a meeting, can you help me?"

"Uh sure what's your friend's name?"

"Carmen Jockolva."

At this Burt ended up dropping all his files all over again.

"Your friend is Carmen Jockolva, the heir to the Jockolva fortune?" he said his voice full of excitement and enthusiasm.

I gave a nervous half laugh, "Umm yup that's her alright."

"Hell yah! I'll take you," he put his scattered files on top of the water cooler and we were on our way.

"Ms. Jockolva is in a board meeting, all board meetings are held in a room in the back," he said straightening his tie.

Carmen was in the process of tapping a pencil against the table when a knock came to the door interrupting someone's presentation. All heads turned toward the sound. A man in a gray striped suit closest to the

Chosen

door turned to answer it, there were some whispers and then the man called out Carmen's name. Carmen was happy for any excuse to get out of that dull setting.

"Excuse me ladies and gentlemen it seems I have an urgent matter to attend to. Please continue. Victor will you take over for me?" she said preparing to leave.

Victor was Vice President of Operations; he was also Carmen's babysitter, as if she didn't know. How else would her mother be getting so much information about her performance at Company meetings and other similar obligations.

Outside of the conference room Carmen was greeted by a soggy Emma, wet from the rain head to toe and her obviously underpaid and eager escort, Burt.

"Hi I'm Burt, it's a pleasure to meet you Ms. Jockolva, I work here at Jockolva Industries. I was simply assisting your friend, Ms. Carter, here in locating you." He said all this while shaking the life out of her arm.

"Well it's also nice to meet you and thank you for showing Emma the way." She said relinquishing his grasp on her hand.

With that Burt regretfully left to attend to other matters.

"Interns don't get paid," said Carmen after he left.

"Huh well no wonder then," I said.

"Come on we can talk in the break room it's just down the hall to the left I'll meet you there in a second," said Carmen.

Carmen reopened the door to the Conference room and poked her head in putting on another charming smile, "Sorry to disrupt your presentation once again, I would just like to inform all of you that I have a pressing family matter therefore will not be available *all* day, thank you," and she shut the door.

Chosen

In the break room I sat munching on coffee and donuts when Carmen walked in.

"This coffee is terrible really, someone ought to do something about it" I said swallowing a mouthful of crumbs.

"Well if it's really that bad why are you drinking it?" asked Carmen, hopping up on the counter and picking up a donut of her own.

"Makes the donuts taste better," I answered with a grin.

"Emma, you're soaked. Did you walk all this way in the rain to tell me how bad our coffee is? Look at you, you're like a walking puddle," she said squeezing water out of my clothes. "I take that back you're a sponge."

"You're getting water everywhere," I said even though I knew she didn't care.

"They'll get over it; you should get out of that jacket."

"Yes mom," I retorted sarcastically.

"I have some dry clothes that I was going to change into after the meeting, you can put those on," said Carmen ignoring my comment.

Carmen waited in the break room while I went in the bathroom to change. We weren't an exact match in size but they would do, at least they were dry. Back in the break room Carmen seemed to be deep in thought.

"Hey, thanks for the clothes, hope you don't mind but I stuffed my wet clothes back in your backpack. Is that ok?" I said entering the room.

"Yeah, that's fine" said Carmen waking from her thoughts.

"Well now that you have the day off how 'bout we get some grub."

At that we both headed downstairs and out the front door lobby but every few minutes or so I would see her glance at me like she had something to say or she wanted to tell me something.

Apparently Carmen was supposed to meet our friend Adam for lunch at Café Don Pablo's so we decided to eat lunch there. As we walked

Chosen

across the puddle stained parking lot of Jockolva Industries Carmen got a call from our other friend Liz telling her to come pick her up. Liz lived about twenty minutes away.

    Liz was found alone when she was five and with no family to claim her was put in foster care. Unfortunately no family was able to control Liz and her unique individuality. This was how she met Carmen, Adam and I, after ten years of moving from foster home to foster home she ran away to New Jersey. After befriending us, she was soon convinced to stop sleeping on the streets and to find a foster family in New Jersey, I even offered to adopt her as a sister.

    Carmen didn't have her own car, her mom wouldn't let her have one; the car Carmen was driving actually belonged to the company. It was a silver Toyota, with leather seats! Technically she wasn't allowed to drive it but what her mother didn't know wouldn't hurt her. While on the way to pick up Liz I started to fiddle with the radio a bit. The sound of static and infomercials soon changed my mind.

    Liz was already waiting by the mailbox when we pulled into her foster parent's driveway.

    "What took so long?" she called, jumping into the backseat along with a few bags.

    "Traffic," I answered. "What's with the bags?"

    "I don't like these parents anymore I want new ones," answered Liz bluntly.

    Liz sat in the middle seat in the back of the silver Toyota, her bags piled up to the right of her. Her jet black hair, with blue streaks cut very short that barely touched her shoulders, still managed to fall across her face. She was unusually pale, not one freckle. Liz's brown eyes stared very intently at the back of the car seat in front of her, revealing nothing. She wore a dark blue jean jacket, matching Capri, a tank top and sneakers. She wore rings on almost every finger, had four bracelets, an anklet, and eight piercings, all of them on her ears and all she had done herself.

    I turned in my seat to look at her, "What do you mean you want new parents?" Carmen wanted to turn in her seat too; however, she managed a questioning yet concerned look through the rearview mirror.

    "You mean you're running away. Why?" called Carmen from the driver's seat.

    "I told you, I don't like them anymore. I figured I'd just chill at one of your guys' place for a while."

    "Liz, your parents wouldn't just let you runaway, do they know you're doing this?" At this she would not look at me. "Liz look at me!"

    "No, and they're not my parents." said Liz.

    I let out a sigh, "Liz" I said sounding exasperated.

    "I'm not going back" she stated matter of fact, and I saw in her face that she spoke nothing but truth. Of course she always did tell the truth, no matter how much it hurt, made me wonder what she would look like if she lied.

    "You can't stay at my place, we're in the process of moving," I told her.

    "You can stay with me, actually that would be great because Caitlyn and Caroline should be returning from their ski trip soon and this way I won't be outnumbered." Carmen offered with a grin. Carmen's sisters were real pieces of work. Their only skill in life was knowing how to be pains in the you know where.

    "Hey, Carmen? I was also wondering if I could stay over too." I asked.

    "Of course, even better." she said.

Chosen

I didn't want to tell her why and she didn't ask; she knew me well enough she didn't have to. For some reason I just can't accept my dad and this new girlfriend of his, they were getting pretty serious and yet I just couldn't stand her.

Forty minutes later the three of us found ourselves in the parking lot of Café Don Pablo's.

"Aaah *finally!* I'm starved" announced Liz stretching as she got out of the car.

"We're late, do you think Adam is still here?" asked Carmen, slamming the car door shut.

Just as I was about to reply that I had no idea; there he was a couple of tables ahead of us. In the outside patio of the café, at a little round table with a red umbrella, sat Adam. He was looking at his watch; it looked like he was just about to leave. We called over to him and he looked up to see us coming.

At the age of sixteen Adam stood at an even six foot. His almond shaped, honey brown eyes looked tired, like he hadn't been sleeping. His dark brown semi longish hair seemed messed up more than usual and looked like it needed to be washed. His clothes, consisting of black jeans, t-shirt, and jacket were somewhat wrinkled.

Seeing us Adam freaked, he bolted over to us managing to knock two chairs out of the way. When he got to us he grabbed me by the shoulders and gave me one of his lung crushing hugs. When he finally let go and I could breath, still holding me by the shoulders he asked me if I was ok.

"Well after a hug like that..." I responded.

I searched his face yet didn't know how to describe what I saw. I saw his eyes, his beautiful eyes and gorgeous long lashes. His strong set chin and that he was in desperate need of a haircut, yet I kind of liked the way his hair always managed to fall across his eyes. But what he was feeling or thinking, I could not tell, he was so guarded, and then I *knew*.

"You *know*", it came out almost a whisper, "How do you know?" I pushed him away. I couldn't look at him. I wanted to run.

"Did they hurt you?" he repeated

Carmen and Liz were on top of me now, crowded around me. They were worried and wanted to know what was going on. Everyone was talking at once, it was just the three of them but I felt surrounded. I needed air.

Sick of being kept in the dark, finally Carmen yelled, "What the hell happened?"

"Snakes. They raided her house last night." answered Adam.

Great now starts the round of hugging, I thought to myself. I needed air.

"Oh Emma, I'm so sorry, you're not hurt are you, why didn't you tell me!" she said while giving me another lung crushing hug followed by Liz.

"Those Snakes should know better than to mess with you cuz I'll beat the crap out of them," said Liz.

"Err that's great Liz but I have to take another breath sometime. But really guys I'm fine, they broke my window, that's it."

I hated this, never really was one for pity parties. Don't get me wrong hugs are great and all but when it's for stuff like this they tend to lose their appeal. I'm supposed to be strong, independent; I'm not supposed to be the one in need of hugs to make me feel better. I will never let pity hugs or the Snakes ever make me feel weak. The only hugs that ever used to make me feel better were my mother's, nonjudgmental, compassionate and gone. She made me feel safe; with her I couldn't be touched.

Chosen

By now we had all ordered and decided to eat inside at a booth. The place was warm and inviting.

"How did you know?" I asked when I had gotten over my surprise, after all I had told no one, as far as I was concerned it never happened; till *he* showed up.

"Uh wha?" answered Adam, his mouth half full of cheeseburger.

"Ugh, gross! Chew with your mouth closed!" said Liz tossing a french fry at him.

"How did you know?" I repeated even louder this time to make sure he would hear me.

"I've got connections," he shrugged and that's all he would say to that.

Conversation soon changed to the sleepover we had planned for tonight and what kind of movies we all wanted to rent. It looked like we were in for an all night junk food bash; pizza and movie marathon.

"Horror!" screeched out Carmen, throwing her arms in the air to show her enthusiasm.

"Romance," Liz announced diplomatically.

I threw in 'comedy', laughter sounded nice. We argued for a few short minutes but we all knew that it would it end up being a little bit of everything so we claimed 'romance' to ensure a long overdue girls night. There was no way Adam was going to be able to crash our party now knowing we would be watching what he referred to as "chic-flicks". Oh no, he was *way* too macho for that. We even had the audacity to pretend to have our feelings hurt that he wouldn't be joining our movie marathon.

"Aaww Adam, are you sure you don't want to watch movies with us?" teased Carmen.

"Yah Adam maybe you'll learn something," Liz laughed at him.

Chosen

"I'm not going anywhere near a bunch of mushy tearjerkers and you crazies." He made it sound like doing so would be giving up and arm and a leg. We all laughed at this, Adam just being Adam. He never failed us; he was someone to rely on, even if it was to call us 'crazy'.

We headed out into the alleyway deciding to walk over to the video store after saying our goodbyes to Adam. The alleyway was dark and dank, making it hard to see. It wasn't raining but water fell off of the fire escapes above us and there were puddles splattered from the morning's rain. I could hear the pit pat splash of our feet on pavement echoing off the narrow alleyway.

We were halfway there when a shadow-like figure caught my attention. About two feet in front of us, it moved swiftly next to the farthest fire escape. What I found strange was that it was there one moment and gone the next. It sort of shimmered and there it was again, the strangeness of it stopped me where I stood. I turned to look beside me wondering if my friends had just seen what I had seen but they had not stopped, they just kept walking.

"Guys wait! Come here, do you see that?"

"Emma what are you doing its frreezing out here, let's go" called Liz.

"Just come here!" I knew it was cold but I wanted them to hurry before whatever it was disappeared again.

"Ok, ok but let's make it quick, what's your issue anyway?" asked Liz.

"What do you see?" I asked pointing towards where I saw the shimmering figure.

"Emma there's nothing there but the fire escape" answered Carmen, a bit impatient now.

Chosen

"So you guys don't see anything?" as I continued to stare at the figure.

"Why, what do you see?" they asked.

The shimmering figure hadn't disappeared again. I could see it perfectly clear. So why was it that I could see it and not them?

"Nothing lets go".

I started walking faster now which pleased Carmen and Liz. Before we knew it the video store was right in front of us.

As we entered the video store, a song was playing on the speakers. 'I'll still follow you home,' was part of the lyrics. It was by one of my favorite bands. After jumping at shadows or, rather seeing shadows jump at me; I would have liked nothing more than anything *but* that song at that moment. It was such a stalker song.

"Let's just get the movies and go okay?" I suggested.

'Just to follow you home.'

Carmen and Liz seemed cool with that idea, splitting in search of their movies', while I headed toward the comedy section.

I scanned the shelves, one video had a picture of a woman covered in mud with two children on either side of her, angelic little smiles lighting up their faces. It was about a woman who discovers the joy of parenting …pass. Why was it, I thought, that comedy felt the need to display children as a form of torture against adults? Not only comedy but children were being used more and more often in horror movies, for a very different reason however. Children have always been seen as the source of pure innocence and seeing pure innocence corrupted or tainted scares people. Now, I didn't know much about parenting, but I did have seven brothers and they were anything *but* innocent.

Chosen

Glancing at another video I saw that it had Jackie Chan in it. It wasn't recent but you could never go wrong with Jackie Chan. (For any of you who have never seen the first *Rush Hour* SHAME ON YOU) In this one he plays a cop, and is teamed up with Chris Tucker who plays a cop from New York in rescuing a little girl in a hostage situation. Then I saw it, "There you are," I said smiling, Abbot and Costello, the real heart of comedy.

Just then Liz and Carmen came striding up arguing over the movies they had picked out. Liz had picked out *The Notebook*, one of the greatest classic love stories of all time, while Carmen had grabbed *Pinocchio's Revenge*. Carmen's theory was in order to watch the movies she picked out you had to have the right personality, and what is the right personality you ask? It's the brilliant combination of horror, suspense, sometimes gore, and the ability to find it all entertaining. In Carmen's opinion horror movies were the easiest to make fun of, and she was right.

We were on our way towards the front to check out when Liz decided to exchange *The Notebook* for a new movie that had just come out that was equally romantic. Liz liked to put on a tough act but when it came to little things like picking out movies it was easy to see inside she was just another scared kid in a messed up world. She believed everyone deserved to be loved. Secretly I believed she did this to make up for all the dead beat foster parents that never loved her, and then instantly hated myself for it. Liz was special. She made you feel special. She loved with all her heart, never asking for anything in return; she was also young and naïve. I didn't want her to turn into me.

The store was closing so the back of the store was completely empty. They had even turned some of the lights off in their eagerness to close. Liz had already grabbed the new movie and was going to put *The*

Chosen

Notebook back where she found it. So she headed toward the back of the store to the section where they had turned off all the lights. The back of the store was completely deserted; everyone was at the front either checking out or getting ready to. After finding the 'N' section on the bottom shelf she found the empty space where she had taken the movie from the shelf and put it back. As she was standing back up, turning around she fell straight back to the floor. It was so quiet back there, strange that she hadn't heard a thing. She put her hand to her chest to calm herself. In her fright she had knocked over one of the shelves so movies were strewn across the floor. Standing before Liz, was a young, very tall, dark skinned boy with gorgeous cheekbones and the cutest dimples she had ever seen.

"Don't you know better than to sneak up on people?" said Liz getting to her feet.

"Sorry, I hadn't meant to scare you," said the boy looking sheepish.

"Correction, you didn't *scare* me, you *startled* me as in I wasn't expecting to turn around and poof suddenly there *you* are, startled, get it?"

"Yeah I get it, look I am sorry," he said flashing a movie star smile, "I was just returning this movie," he held it up as if for proof. It was *Night of the Living Dead.*

Whoever he was, he had an accent, sounded Brazilian.

"Mhmm. So you're a zombie man huh? I'm more into things that don't come back to life after it's dead, if you catch my drift.

He laughed, "Yeah I guess you could say that, by the way my name is Fu."

"Elizabeth," she replied shaking his hand.

Liz was pleased at how interested he seemed to be in her. His eyes never left hers for a second. She would have thought it was creepy except he seemed so friendly.

Chosen

"Fu? What kind of name is that?" questioned Liz

"A long story which I would love to tell you sometime," replied Fu laughing again.

"Well Elizabeth, I know I *startled* you but to tell the truth I'm glad I did. It has been really nice talking to you. Maybe we could do this again some time?" He looked around the store as if he had forgotten he was there. "Well, you know what I mean. You, me, a movie, minus the store, how about it?" he gave her another award winning smile.

"Yeah maybe," she answered then realized he was waiting for her to give him her number. "Give me your hand," she said. He did so obediently. Pulling out a pen she scratched a number onto his palm. "If you ever feel like giving me a call you can reach me here."

"I'll call you, Elizabeth," said Fu; he seemed to like the sound of her name.

"That's what they all say," said Liz, starting to walk away.

"Liz, how long does it take for you to put away a movie? The store is about to close let's go!" said Carmen grabbing her arm and steering her towards checkout.

"I met a guy," said Liz.

"You mean *that* guy?" said Carmen pointing to a rugged guy near the entrance of the video store; a man with a gold medallion around his neck, shaggy dirty blond hair and scruffy beard. Along with some raggedy clothes, he looked like a regular hobo. The guy had no style at all really, that stupid clunky medallion around his neck looked utterly ridiculous and he could really use a shower.

"Eww no, the guy I met was in the back of the store and he's not a creepy hobo; he should be right behind me," said Liz, looking around.

Chosen

"Liz, there's no one back there, who you see right now is all that's left," I told her.

"No, that's impossible; the front door is the only way out, you had to have seen him. Tall hottie, probably Brazilian; sound familiar?" probed Liz.

By now we had paid for our movies and were on our way out with Liz still trying to convince us her mysterious stranger was real. "Ya'll had to have seen him, ya'll must be lying, this isn't funny," said Liz, convinced of sabotage. This is certainly something we would do, however in this case we could plead innocent. In Liz's frustration a slight southern accent surfaced, as it did on many occasions; where it came from however no one knew for Liz had spent her entire life in the city. "Liz, if anyone's lying it's you because we did not see this guy of whom you speak." I said as we began to pull into Carmen's driveway. "Whoa," said Liz, her comeback forgotten.

"What?"

"Nothing, it's just bigger than I remember," explained Liz, looking at the house as if she were a tourist. It was a two story house, three if you counted the basement. The steps of the house started at the front then rounded all the way around towards the back. Black and white painted brick enclosed the entire outer wall of the house. The entryway was shielded by two French columns. "It was built by my grandfather before he died," said Carmen.

"The place is completely dark. Is anyone even here?" I asked.

"Relax I have the keys, and I don't know, Caitlyn and Caroline should be back from their ski trip, unfortunately," answered Carmen.

Walking in the side door, the kitchen floor shone like the stars on a summer's night. Liz tossed her bags on the counter along with the movies. "Yo, I vote brownies," I said as I started grabbing a box from the cabinet.

Chosen

Carmen then took it from me and began reading the directions, tossing it back she added, "And I vote that you make them."

"Eeeeww what are *they* doing here?" It was Caitlyn and Caroline, the '*they*' they were referring to was Liz and me, although they were not too fond of Carmen either.

"*They* are staying over so get over it *fast*," said Carmen. Liz stuck her tongue out just for spite. Being the major skanks that they were and not wanting to let up so easily, Caitlyn and Caroline stooped so low as to spill coffee all over Liz's bags, not the least bit sneaky. Carmen and I had to hold Liz back. That is one fifteen year old you do not want to piss off, yet in this case I was extremely tempted to just let her have at it. "Ya'll wanna mess with me? Bring it! Come on, let's go!" She leapt at them but she wasn't close enough to get in a good swing before Carmen and I caught her. We watched them walk away their gleeful little smiles plastered to their faces as if they've won something; "That's right bitches smile, I know where you sleep," said Liz still trying to fight us off until they were out of sight. "Your sister's are skank whores," said Liz after she had calmed down. "I'm adopted, I swear it," said Carmen. "We know," I told her. "Let's get started watching the movies," I said as we cleaned up Liz's bags for her. "Liz go ahead and toss your bags in my room," said Carmen. "I'll go ahead and start the brownies alright," I said pulling a pan from the hidden compartment beneath the stove.

I started mixing the brownies, while Carmen and Liz went to get pj's on. Carmen and Liz both managed to swipe some chocolate from the bowl as I swatted at them with the spoon meanwhile getting chocolate splattered across Liz's face.

The basement was one of our many treasured haunts. We called it our "cave". I plopped myself on the floor in the space between the couch and

Chosen

TV, my coveted position. The basement consisted of a couch, two chairs, and of course where would humongous houses be without their flat screen TVs. Carmen had movies but we always had more fun renting them. I rested my head against the back of the couch, wondering who would win the "My movie first" debate. Carmen liked it when we came over, not that she ever wouldn't; she simply said we made the house feel more "lived in." For some reason I read a lot more into those words than I had meant to. I knew Carmen got lonely and that we were all she really had. And that she thought her mom was a total psycho witch and could go fall in a hole. Her sisters were a *whole* other story; brain dead losers, stuck up witches who spend their money on useless crap. If any of them were ever home at all then I would *want* to be alone however, I guess being stuck with an empty house isn't all that cool either. Blood doesn't mean anything to her though. We're her family. Liz knows exactly how Carmen feels of course. Sometimes I wonder if they hate me for having a family but I know they don't. Any family is better than none right? Wrong. My family is not as bad as you may presume it to be. Unlike Liz and Carmen who get lonely, I find myself suffocating. I have a very large family I need my space, yet everywhere I turn *more brothers*! Also, my dad is always trying to talk to me, and I love him, but I can't stand talking to him. I know that's awful and you probably won't understand. It's just after my mom died it hurt to talk to him, it hurt to care. Is it silly to think that I might lose him too-and if so then why am I unconsciously trying to protect my heart when I know the only thing it will do is leave guilt in the long run. I decided to call my dad. He wouldn't care if I was here, probably hasn't even noticed yet. I dialed his number and waited as it rang.

    "Hello?" It was Tarrasa, "Hey it's Emma, is my dad there?" suddenly a bit irritated.

Chosen

"Oh! Hey is that your daddy's new girlfriend? Can I talk to her?" Liz, a concoction stirring up from inside her head, started reaching for the phone but I pulled it away before she could grab it. "What? Now you need privacy to talk on the phone around us?" she yelled as I decided to walk out to the patio sliding doors. "Apparently," sticking my head back through the sliding glass door I yelled back, giving Liz an accusing look.

"Emma?" it was my dad this time.

"Yeah Dad it's me, I'm over at Carmen's house, look I know I said that I would come over later but is it ok if I stay over?"

"Yeah sure sweetie, just make sure to bring the rest of your stuff by the house tomorrow, the door's locked, but the key is under the mat." I don't think I'll need a key I thought to myself; they obviously hadn't notice the broken window. "Thanks Dad that'll work out great, I will see you tomorrow." He said goodbye and we hung up.

I went inside just in time for the movie debate climax. I decided to sit back and enjoy the show. Carmen had just finished explaining her reasons behind picking scary movies first. Of course, if it were up to Carmen she would probably prefer an all night horror movie fiesta. According to Carmen horror movies being the first choice is actually for Liz's benefit. Watching the horror movie first would get it over with instead of prolonging it," She said, holding up *Pinocchio's Revenge* as if it would help.

"Normally, Carmen I would agree with you, – snort (what? who did that?) but I've never seen this movie and I really want to see it," replied Liz.

Well, if we're doing the whole "save the best for last" routine then which should we pick? *Pinocchio's Revenge* because it really is the best or the new movie because you think it is better?" retorted Carmen.

I broke it up before round three could begin. "Hey who wants to come with me to my house real quick?"

Chosen

Surprisingly I had two volunteers with no complaints, and they hadn't even asked why we were going yet. I smiled to myself. I loved my family. We packed into Carmen's company car all done up in our finest pj's but also nice and cozy. I wore my favorite lounge pants, flip flops, a tank top and a jacket. Carmen wore an over large sweatshirt and bootie shorts, I warned them it was cold but of course no one listens to me. Liz had her short black hair up in chopsticks and wore a sweater, along with giant pink bunny slippers. (So that's where those went) "So, are you going to tell us why were going to your house?" asked Liz.

"Yup, I was just waiting to see how long it would take one of you to ask." Liz rolled her eyes at this. "I left some boxes in my old house, I don't want them getting stolen," I answered.

"And this couldn't wait till morning?" asked Carmen.

"Do you have something better to do?" I inquired.

"Yes! Brownies and movie marathon back *that* way," said Liz pointing in the opposite direction.

"You guys were not even close to picking a movie. We had at least another hour of negotiating." I retorted, shutting them both up. I love how once we're in the car that they start to complain. Two minutes later we we're pulling into the driveway of my old house.

It was small but I had lived there all my life and it had never seemed small until just now. Maybe I had finally out grown it, if that's possible; I wasn't entirely sure.

I grabbed the key from under the mat. Walking in I just felt *so* utterly *empty,* so many memories yet what was left of those memories seemed almost lost in this house that had become such an empty void for it was now a blank canvass ready for future families and new memories. In the end is all we're left with is memories? The place was dark, abandoned.

Chosen

Shadows danced across the walls creating illusions. This place is kind of creepy at night; of course I would never admit that out loud.

I grabbed two boxes and headed back out to the car, leaving Carmen and Liz to grab the rest. I was on my way out the front door when I managed to drop both boxes in a crash. No more than sixty feet in front of me at the end of the drive way stood the creepy hobo from the video store. The man with the gold medallion, shaggy dirty blond hair and scruffy beard just stood there looking up at the front door at me. Hearing the crash, Carmen and Liz ran to see what had happened. What the heck was he doing here? I thought to myself.

"Who's that?" asked Liz as she came up behind me.

He started walking up the drive way toward us. The gold medallion around his neck was glistening in the night with a hypnotizing gleam.

"That's the creepy hobo from the video store, I don't like this. Get back inside," I said pushing Liz backwards and shutting the door behind me.

"What's he doing here?" asked Liz.

"You wanna go ask him?" I said sarcastically, locking the door. Carmen looked at me disapprovingly. I rolled my eyes, now wasn't a good time for a lesson in manners. Somehow I just sensed that whoever he was and whatever he wanted, it wasn't harmless. This was no ordinary hobo. The hairs on the back of my neck prickled with an uneasiness that I was sure Carmen and Liz felt too. I was about to tell them to go out the back door when a loud bang sounded, the front door flew off pummeling me to the ground, and landing on top of Liz pinning her to the floor. The hobo walked in stepping over the debris.

Although we were unconscious, he bent low so that even if we hadn't been pummeled into the floor we would be able to hear him, "Hello angels, I've been looking for you," he said smiling.

Chosen

Carmen had been knocked to the ground, however she remained perfectly unharmed. Once standing, Carmen charged full force at their intruder. "Aaah I see there is one left standing. I shall deal with you," he said calmly as Carmen headed straight toward him. Just as she was about to knock him to the ground, she froze in mid leap then suddenly she could no longer move.

"Let's go for a drive shall we?" he said stroking his beard.

Chapter 4

My head felt like it was about to explode, everything was blurry. I realized I was in what looked to be an old warehouse. My wrist hurt like crazy and I saw that this was because I was chained to an iron rod. Next to me was Liz. She was already awake. Her expression said anger, defiance, a look that said if you touch me I'll rip you apart, but I knew better. I could see the fear in her eyes. I knew because she stole that look from me, except for the fear, I have no fear. "Liz, where is Carmen?"

She turned to me her expression immediately relaxing as she saw me, "I don't know, when I woke up you were unconscious and I didn't see Carmen, do you think there is a chance she got away?"

I sighed, "No, Carmen would never leave us." Well crap I thought.

"Emma," said Liz

"Yeah?"

"I'm glad you're awake," I gave her a reassuring smile.

"What do you think he wants with us?" she asked.

I said the first thing that came to mind and the only thing that made sense, "Liz, Carmen is a millionaire; this guy is just a coward working on another 'get rich quick scheme.'"

"Mhmm ransom," she mumbled, more to herself than me, acknowledging that this proposition made sense to her. She had forgotten that Carmen was a millionaire but I didn't say anything; I understood. I had moments like that often even when we went to her house it stopped dawning on me that she was up to her ears in money, probably because I practically lived there myself. Now it only took moments like these to remind me how very different Carmen's life really was from ours.

Chosen

"Here comes Carmen!" I said eager with worry and wanting to know what to expect next. "Along with him," it came out almost a growl. He chained her up next to us, "Are you ok? What did he do to you?" I whispered to her.

"Relax I didn't hurt her," he said wrapping the chains around her wrists.

"I wasn't talking to you!" I snarled.

"Mhmm feisty for someone chained to a bar," he said amused.

"Emma, he didn't hurt me," said Carmen.

I looked at her, I was glad she was ok, but now completely confused, "What do you want with us?"

"I could tell you but what fun would that be?" he said grinning. "Now you're next," he said pointing to Liz.

"Touch me and you die," she said glaring at him.

I gripped the pole above me, lifting myself up and kicking off the wall behind me I swung at his head and gave him a good solid kick in the face. "Looks like someone is eager to go next," he said standing back up and holding his jaw. He undid my chains and I fell to the floor. Dropping from what had to be at least four feet off the ground I braced myself for the impact of the cold concrete yet to my surprise two seconds after my release I found I had landed on my feet perfectly unscathed.

It looked like the warehouse was an old abandoned machine factory used to cut and transport steel. "I give you my word you shall not be harmed," he said as he watched my eyes scanning for escape routes. Obliviously he didn't take kidnapping into account. Hanging out in a dusty old warehouse was not what I had in mind for tonight, and what kind of hobo says 'shall' anyway? Who the heck is this guy?

Chosen

He walked over to a backroom that looked like it used to be an office. He opened the door waiting for me to follow and to my gut wrenching disgust, I did. The room held a dusty table and two chairs. There were no windows, the only light came from a crooked light fixture. He shut the door behind us. The wallpaper was torn with what looked to be faded sailboats. The dust made my eyes itch, it was evident we were the only people who'd been in here in years. He took a seat on the table offering me a chair causing the dust to billow out from under him and me to sneeze. "That's a beautiful necklace" He said. There was silence. What did he want me to do, thank him? "It's very symbolic," he continued. Absentmindedly I stroked my necklace as he spoke. It was a half-crescent moon shape with the two beads attached at the knot above the crescent. My mother had given it to me. After she died I never took it off. "The two beads that dangle beside your crescent moon represent balance and power, and I don't know if you can see it but beneath the surface of your crescent moon there should be an image of an eye." He stated calm and informative, patiently awaiting my response. My eyes grew wide but I quickly recovered. How did he know about the eye?

His calmness unnerved me. He looked to be about 6'2 and 280 lbs. give or take, he obliviously hadn't showered in weeks. He seemed to be the type of guy that knew he could use his sheer mass bodyweight to intimidate people. What surprised and unnerved me was that he didn't have that effect on me. He seemed to recognize that he didn't have to be threatening for others to know he was intimidating, his size spoke for itself. I wasn't sure if I should be more or less frightened at this fact. His words rose barely above a whisper yet in them I could not help but feel an underlying threat. I felt as if I moved or even breathed the wrong way I would be creating even more agitation and heaviness to this small dusty room.

Chosen

"Who are you?" I had stopped playing with my necklace.

"My name is of no consequence," he replied.

"Why are we here?" I asked, surprised he was letting me interrogate him.

"Why do you think you are here?" he questioned back.

"Enough games you're just toying with us!" At this point I was on my feet practically screaming at him.

"Sit down," he commanded in that whispery growl. "You will get your answers as soon as I get mine. Now I'm curious, why do you believe I have brought you all here?"

"Ransom," it came out a question. He grinned something fierce with a sparkle in his eye.

"Good guess my dear but if I were asking for ransom you would be dead already." It took me a few seconds before I realized I had been holding my breath. He sighed, "I'll explain, you see logically I would have only taken the rich girl, however the two of you intervened and considering both of you had seen my face I would have disposed of you quickly. Now aren't you glad that I am not interested in ransom?" he inquired.

I had to ask, "What *are* your intentions?"

He got off the table, taking the second chair and turning it so that it was not facing me. "Well, I do believe it is story time. It all starts long ago before man walked the Earth. Demons and creatures of many shapes, sizes, forms and such unbearable cruelty that I pray the earth never tastes again. Every living thing has a life source he explained. The Earth being life, one and of itself, its life began to diminish; drowning in blood and chaos. Seeing this, the gods intervened, sending the creatures back from whence they came by bending the fabric of space and time to an alternate universe, so very foreign from our own. He soon began to lose himself in his words, his eyes portraying a far off expression. The Great God Orion forced all of them off this world where they could no longer wreak destruction and havoc on Earth, sealing the portal of their world behind them so that they may never return and in turn restoring balance to the Universe.

"And they all lived happily ever after THE END."

His brows furrowed disapprovingly, "No interruptions," he snarled.

I ignored him, "So if the portal was closed then why the story?" Not that I believed any of this for a second.

He gave me another stern look before he continued. "Because dear child the portal reopened, they returned and Orion was no longer there to stop them." What did this story have to do with me and my friends I wondered? "It is my theory," he continued, "that the demons could smell, sense the newfound blood that seeped into the Earth's core and hungered for it. It is this hunger for blood, violence, for *more*; that I believe was somehow able to help them escape from their world and into ours. The portal had reopened; with Orion's death the three sons equally took their place at the throne."

The scent of metal, sweat, and soap filled Liz's nose as she twisted and wiggled uselessly chained to an iron rod. Carmen was far enough that Liz was unable to reach her. Ignoring the pain in her wrist she slowly forced it through the chains, gently at first then harder. It was as if she was still at home trying to persuade the lid off of a pickle jar, slowly but once it started to give away she yanked it free! With her now bloodied hand she reached back pulled one of the chopsticks out of her hair. Using it she managed to manipulate the chains to her advantage. They soon fell to the floor in a loud CLANG. At the last second before falling to the floor with the chains she grabbed hold of the iron rod to ease herself down. "I don't know how Emma did it but I'd rather not be chop suey". Emma had fallen straight to the ground with ease.

He stretched, wrinkling his nose as he stirred the dust. Sitting back down he continued on, "Here comes the part you've been waiting for; the reason you're all here. The three brothers, he continued, created reincarnates of them using a *citizens spell*, the same spell used to create servant gods. Anyway these three warriors were sent to Earth's aid many years ago. However, though created by gods they were not invincible. When one died, their powers would roam the Earth in search of the next heir."

"Nice story, what do you want?" I interrupted, clearly unimpressed. What a looney, I thought to myself.

"My medallion has the power to locate such powers." The corner of one side of his mouth twitched in amusement. I was confused; I thought this guy was nuts in the beginning but now he was just plain psycho. "I'm sorry to say I lied to you Emma. I promised no harm would come to you, but unfortunately your powers are already upon you and I cannot take your power from you without there being a negative impact, it's just not possible. If your powers had not come just yet like your friends then perhaps, but unfortunately…"

Anger washed through me like a wave. "I don't know who you think you are but I'm leaving and I'm taking my friends with me." I went for the door.

"You've been seeing things, things you can't explain like that shadow in the alley? It was real, all of it" he said standing up to block the door.

"I'm leaving," I repeated, now seriously freaked out. I leapt over the table and ran straight for the door. I threw my arms over my head before

Chosen

I slammed face first into wood. I heard the door split open from the impact and when I opened my eyes I found myself outside against the far wall. My arms were incased in armor. As soon as I regained myself I got up to run, with psycho hobo at my heels.

"Alright genius what now?" asked Liz after tossing her a chopstick and helping Carmen down. "Thanks, let's go get Emma." she replied, rubbing her wrist to ease to the pain. "They're somewhere in the back of the warehouse, that much we know." She said running towards the back. It was then that Carmen and Liz nearly ran over Emma as she was running out of an office. Liz saw the hobo not far behind her. Quickly she grabbed a crowbar and waiting till Emma passed by her she swung the crowbar at him as hard as she could, dropping it as they ran.

"Emma, are you alright!" asked Liz out of breath. Emma had pulled her sleeves down to cover the armor encasing her arms.

"I'm fine," I retorted. No one said anything else until they were out of the warehouse and at least three blocks of zigzagging and fence jumping.

"Do you think it is safe?" asked Liz.

"He knows where we live," said Carmen "Where are we supposed to go?" They sat on the curb still out of breath but too afraid to stay in one place for too long.

He stood slowly and painfully a large bruise already beginning to form. He had at least one broken rib. The feeling of cold cement tickled his skin. A thousand sharp knives, pins and needles entered his brain forcing him to reel in agony and lose consciousness yet again. He awoke to blackness, it engulfed him. Images swirled around like a whirlwind. Standing he let his vision clear, the images coming closer into view. It suddenly dawned on him, these images were his memories. Pictures of his past flashed before his eyes one after another. The first image was of him and his father. He found himself in the library of the institute where he grew up. He could smell the leather binding, candle wax and dust; it felt so real and yet there he was standing there staring at his younger self and his father who had died many years before. "I know who you are Nova," said a voice that echoed through the darkness.

"Who are you!" he said with more courage than he actually felt.

Stay away from the Angels, Nova," said the voice, "Or I'll kill you. This is your last and only warning Nova, do you understand? Their powers belong to me."

Chapter 5

"Come on in," said Adam. He watched as the three of us crowded in the doorway taking his arm off the doorframe to let us through. "Got bored of your movies and decided to find me for some real entertainment I see." He said walking to the kitchen table to pour him some coffee.

"I know it is late." I said surprised he was even awake and not wanting to ask if we had woke him.

"You guys can take my room, I'll take the couch." He sipped his coffee. I started to say something but stopped. After all that is why we came and I was tired. Although I was in no mood for questions, I was surprised he didn't ask.

Liz headed toward the bathroom, shifting through the cabinets in order to find a bandage for her wrist. Carmen was the first to claim Adam's twin sized mattress, curling up into the soft cotton sheets scattered with the Batman emblem. She smiled to herself, hugging a pillow, letting her exhaustion finally take over she fell asleep almost instantly. I walked in; Carmen was snoring gently; grabbing a pillow off the bed I tossed it to the floor.

Liz came in behind me, "What are you doing?" she asked.

"You two can take the bed I'll take the floor," I replied.

"Emma are you sure you're alright?" she questioned. I didn't have an answer for that, my mind hadn't even fully processed what had happened. For all I knew it had just been a really bad dream, then I saw Liz's now bandaged wrist and frowned. I hugged her. "Good night Liz."

"Good night," she replied.

I walked into the kitchen; Adam was still awake, "Couldn't sleep?" I inquired, leaning against the countertop. He looked at me as if deciding whether or not to answer, "Bad dreams" he replied, downing another shot of caffeine. "Coffee's not going to help," I said, taking his cup and placing it in the sink, "Thanks for letting us stay here." "You are always welcome," he said, "but why are you here Emma?"

"We were in the neighborhood," I said starting to head back to his room.

He stood blocking my path. He was near enough that I could smell his cologne, "Don't lie to me Emma it doesn't suit you, was it the Snakes, did they hurt you?"

If I lied to him again he'd be angry, if I told him the truth he would be angry. I decided to tell the truth, "We were kidnapped but we got away and we're fine," I said. He was speechless I could see from his expression a thousand questions flying through his head. I wasn't ready to answer questions just yet. "Adam I'm tired I am going to bed," I said and he let me pass.

"I'm sorry," was all he said but in his voice I felt such sincerity that Adam had never dared show before.

When Emma was out of eye sight Adam smashed his fist into the nearest wall. It stung but he barely felt it, pain was a distraction from his thoughts, the anger he felt and the guilt of not being able to prevent what Emma had just told him.

The light in Adam's room was off by now. I could hear the sound of both Carmen and Liz snoring. I felt through the darkness not wanting to bump into anything. Finding my pillow I lowered myself to the floor waiting for sleep to overtake me. As I began to concede to darkness I felt my arms, they were my arms, nothing more, maybe I had imagined it.

Chapter 6

The next morning I awoke to the noon day sun, it was almost 12:00. "Morning sunshine," it was Carmen.

I groaned; my neck was stiff from lying on the floor. I stood stretching, "Ugh why didn't you guys wake me?"

"Liz is still asleep and Adam went out for breakfast, I don't think he got any sleep" said Carmen.

"Today is Monday," I said, suddenly realizing that we had skipped school.

"Just think of it as a sick day," Carmen smiled.

We walked into the kitchen. I was in desperate need for some coffee. Unfortunately there wasn't a coffee ground in sight. "Emmy, Carmen!" it was Logan. He came running into the kitchen arms open demanding to be picked up. I scooped him up and swung him round and round. Logan was three years old, Adam's little brother. Their mother died in a shooting accident a year ago; one of those wrong place, wrong time situations. Adam had taken care of Logan ever since. He came up to my knees his dark blond hair and brown eyes peering up at me in earnest. He looked nothing like Adam, I thought to myself.

"Hey buddy, don't you think it's a little early to be bouncing all over the place?" I said lifting him and setting him up on the countertop.

"But Aunt Emmy it's almost noon." he said as Carmen commenced to wipe the sticky juice that seemed to coat the majority of his face. He smiled up at me; it was Adam's smile, something I hadn't seen in awhile.

"Your brother will be home in a bit. Why don't you go and wake Aunty Liz?" We soon heard the sound of Liz groaning in annoyance. Then the sounds of Logan's high pitched squeals of laughter as Liz tickled him

Chosen

into submission. Liz came walking into the kitchen with Logan trailing behind her. "Coffee," groaned Liz, still half asleep.

"Good morning to you too, we're out of coff…," I started as Liz was pouring herself a cup. "How…what?" I was baffled. I swore that just a moment ago when I myself was in search of coffee that there was none to be found.

I was left to my thoughts as Adam came strolling through the doorway arms full of donuts. "Ah, I see you vampires finally decided to join the living."

We swarmed him like vultures who had found their prey. "I call sprinkle!" claimed Liz.

"Carmen, your arm, you're bleeding." It was Adam; he had grabbed a cloth and was headed her way. Carmen watched in fascination as the shiny red fluid dripped across her arm.

"I hadn't noticed," said Carmen.

"This is a big scratch," he said as he applied pressure to her wound, "how did this happen?"

"Must have been the rosebushes we ran through last night," suggested Liz. Just then the sound of someone knocking on the door filled the kitchen.

"Open up! I know you're in there." The voice was thick and husky. The sound of his fist banging against the door made it obvious that he was no small fry. Adam went to the door. Standing before him was a boy. Tall, broad shouldered, his hair was dirty blond cut so that his hair just touched his ears. Eyes shining like the sea. The light from the doorway gave the impression that he was glowing. He had the face of an avenging angel for his eyes screamed of anger and his face was twisted into a grimace. Adam towered over him like he was nothing. His dark brown hair made him look like a dark serene angel. I weaseled my way past Adam.

"What do you want?" I questioned.

His faced softened at the sight of me. "I called you; you didn't answer so I got worried."

I pulled the door shut behind me and walked outside. I knew the others didn't like him and I didn't want Derik to have to deal with that. He touched my face. His hands were cool and rough, the evidence of hard work. I knew the strength behind them and yet they were surprisingly gentle; like a cuddly bear, only huge. We had been walking; I realized we had walked about half-way down the block. The air was cool and a slight breeze had begun to wake the leaves. Most of the houses in this neighborhood were old so they still had a bit of that Victorian feel. This was tainted by the sight of grass and plants that had devoured most of the yards. The so called sidewalk we walked on was either overlapped by grass or cracked. Adam's neighborhood lay just outside the city so any money that came in was put towards factories, transportation, and so on. Another downside was the pollution that towered over the neighborhood.

For the last couple of minutes Derik had been trying to very discretely reach for my hand, failing miserably. I ignored his attempts.

"Emma." Derik had stopped walking to turn and look at me. "I'm sorry," he said.

I looked at him. He was gorgeous. I turned and resumed walking.

"Emma!" he barked. He grabbed my arm, turning me so that I faced him.

"We're over Derik." I kept my voice even. He wasn't sorry. He was never sorry. His face contorted, revealing a surge of rage and annoyance. I turned to head back to the house. Derik held me, his arm clamped onto me

Chosen

like steel. Most girls would have slapped him, but I'm not like most girls. I slung my free arm back shaping it into a fist. I swung, connected, and watched as he collapsed almost immediately onto the sidewalk. I stepped back in surprise. My fist and arm were encased in a bronzed tinted armor.

I turned on my heel, making a mad dash to the house. I sprinted up the steps two at a time, then stopped. I didn't want to go in yet. I leaned against the doorway out of breath, slinking to the ground. The cool concrete felt good. My head was spinning. What had just happened? Minutes felt like seconds. I sat there just watching the clouds pass overhead. I fell backwards as the door opened, my head thumping against the floor. "Hi," I grinned looking up at Liz.

"We're going back to Carmen's to get our stuff, you coming?"

"Yeah," I answered getting to my feet. I was ready to get out of my pj's. I met everyone outside.

"Hold up!" It was Adam. He sat on his front steps straightening the wrinkle out of Logan's shirt. Adam bent down to Logan's level. "Hey buddy how about we take you over to hang out with Aunt Peg? Hmm?" Peg was their neighbor. She was a nice lady who liked kids. She had known Adam when he was just a boy and although she knew his age she did not give him away. Adam was only sixteen; legally to be able to take care of Logan he had to be eighteen. For Logan to end up in foster care would break both their hearts.

Logan's face lit up immediately, "Aunt Peggy?" he questioned excitedly.

"Aunt Peggy," Adam nodded, steering Logan towards their neighbors' house.

We waited, leaning against Adam's red 1990 Chevy blazer. "Ok, let's go." said Adam, strolling up the driveway; keys jangling in his hand.

Chosen

Just as we had hopped in and began pulling out of the driveway Carmen's cell phone rings. It was her mother. We could hear the sound of her high pitched screeching, a noise that somehow passed for a voice.

"Is everything alright?" questioned Liz. Carmen sighed in that nonchalant way of hers. "It's always something with her, you know how it is." She trailed off. We drove past Big Bill's BBQ, Anna's Hair Salon, and other various department stores and restaurants until buildings slowly began to dwindle as Adam turned onto a back road. Soon we were cruising along Starlit Avenue. A moment later and Adam was easing us into the driveway.

The kitchen was a mess. Cabinets had been left open and chocolate encased the countertops. Next to the stove was a severely charred pan holding what was supposed to be a batch of brownies. Liz walked to it, poking it as if she were contemplating dissection. Carmen reached for it, tossing it into the garbage, pan and all.

"I'm taking a shower" she announced, heading towards her room. Considering Carmen's house had three bathrooms, we followed suit. Adam headed for the basement, our cave; a really pimped out cave. Out of habit he snatched up the remote, throwing himself onto the couch.

The water was warm and refreshing, exactly what I needed. I took my time in the shower allowing the water to cleanse me. When I was finished I wiped the steam free from the mirror. I stared at the reflection the little circle of mirror gave me. I had strawberry blond curly hair that reached to my mid back. I hated my curls. They were so annoying. I wish I had straight hair like Liz. I leaned in closer to inspect my teeth, super long eyelashes and blue eyes. "Gah!" I said out loud, speaking to my reflection. Was that a zit? I groaned. Wrapping a towel around me I headed towards Carmen's room where I had left my stuff. Upon entering I found Carmen and Liz already dressed and waiting for me. Liz sat on Carmen's bed attempting

Chosen

to comb out Carmen's unruly mess of hair, spraying herself with water droplets from her comb in the process. Carmen's hair was not curly like mine but was very thick. I found Liz's bag of clothes and picked out my favorite outfit of her's for the day. A pair of black jeans, my favorite t-shirt, and boots. Liz and I were an exact match in size. The only part of her wardrobe that didn't always fit was her pants. Liz was a lot shorter than me so sometimes some of her pants were too short. Carmen was busy with the hair straightener when Liz had finished combing out her hair. I didn't feel like straightening my hair today so I decided to leave it curly. I plopped onto Carmen's bed waiting for them to finish their hair and makeup. When Liz was done hogging the mirror I borrowed her makeup kit. "You guys realize we have two guest rooms," said Carmen, finishing her hair. "Yeah but that's no fun," answered Liz. I dabbed on some blue eye shadow to make my eyes stand out, eye liner and mascara. I never used foundation although it would have gotten rid of my freckles. "Besides we're already finished." I grabbed my skate board; I had left it at Carmen's weeks ago. Now that we were finished we headed to the basement to get Adam.

"Alright sleeping beauty, let's go!" broadcasted Liz, plopping down onto Adam and producing a loud harrumph.

"I was awake," he growled.

"Good let's go," she said hopping up.

He stretched, "Where are we going?"

"I'm going to the library," said Carmen.

We turned to face her, "Why," I asked.

"I don't need a reason to go to the library," she answered.

"But you have one don't you." I looked at her and she looked away; there was something she wasn't telling me. "This is about last night isn't it?

Chosen

Carmen that man was psychotic, he was speaking gibberish. We do not have magic powers and we are not destined to save the world!"

"I know," she snapped. "This is just something I need to do, ok?" sounding a bit defensive. With Carmen's decision to go to the library we had all decided to go with her.

"What did that guy say to you?" asked Liz, totally confused.

"Nothing Liz, he was just a crazy old man," I answered.

We pulled into the parking lot and found that the library was closed. I stepped out of the car, "It's **Monday**. The library shouldn't be closed." The sign on the door listed the hours.

Mon-Thurs 9:00am-5:00pm

Fri-Sun 12:00pm-5:00pm

Despite the listed hours, the library was closed. This was the only public library within the city limits. "Oh well, ok, ah how bout we head on back to Carmen's and hang out?" suggested Adam.

Around the side of the building a security guard headed to his car. His grey hair produced a horseshoe shape on his balding head. Jangling his keys, he shuffled across the parking lot and was about to enter his car when Carmen called over to him.

"Sir! Sir! Do you work here?" she ran over to him.

At the sound of her voice the man stopped and turned. "Huh? What?" the old man huffed.

"Do you work at the library?" she asked.

"Yeah I do, is there a problem?" he questioned.

"Why is it closed and can you let us in?"

"The library is closed today."

"We can see that, but why is it closed?" asked Adam.

47

Chosen

"Look kids I don't make the rules I just enforce them. Why don't you run along home, come back tomorrow," answered the security guard. The guard watched us, waiting for us to leave. I had a hunch he was the only security the library had and he was eager to leave. We waited a good fifteen minutes for the old man to leave. We hid behind a few parked cars in the lot. After the purr of his engine had faded and could no longer be heard we stepped out from our hiding place.

"Why don't we just come back tomorrow like the man said?" asked Adam.

"That is a good question Adam," said Liz, "But since we're already here we might as well go in." she pulled out her lock picking kit. "A minute tops," she informed us. She jiggled and fidgeted until there was a click. Lock picking was a very useful skill, one of the million reasons we were glad to have Liz around. Not that we made breaking and entering a habit or anything. "Let's go," said Liz obviously proud of herself.

"Tell me again why we just broke into a library!" hissed Adam.

"You guys did not have to come," said Carmen.

"That does not answer my question, and of course we had to come," argued Adam.

"Adam's right, you would still be on the front steps if it weren't for me," said Liz.

"What do you expect to find?" I questioned.

"Will everyone, please just shut up," growled Carmen, exasperated.

We decided to split up. A few minutes later I found myself browsing through rows upon rows of books. I saw a few paint cans by the wall maybe they had closed for renovations. I would stop every once in awhile when a book caught my interest. I was skimming through the fiction section when I stopped to flip through a book titled, 'Wicked', it was a twist

Chosen

off of 'The Wizard of Oz.' With book in hand I continued my search, what I was looking for exactly, I had no clue. Eventually I ended up between the Historic section and the Religious section. Two of which were my least favorite subjects. I was about to leave when I saw something out of the corner of my eye. It gleamed and shimmered, but when I turned to look there was nothing there. It was a large book on the bottom shelf. When I turned to look for it I couldn't see it but, when I turned my head it reappeared. I could only see it in my peripheral vision. I bent low to the ground; it was a large old leather bound manuscript. Although when I looked straight at it I could not see it; I reached for where I knew it was. My hand began to tingle and I felt the book in my hand. It shimmered and finally materialized. It looked as if it hadn't been touched in years. The pages were thick with age.

"Carmen, Adam, Liz, quick come here I found something." It wasn't long before they all found me; crowding around my ancient find. I blew the dust off the cover. It was titled, 'Chosen.'

"There's something strange about that book, I can feel it," said Liz.

"Well open it," said Adam impatiently. Slowly I pulled the pages apart with a loud thud.

Quick as a flash I was blinded by an encompassing display of light. Everything felt so open like I wasn't me, I was floating. I could not get a grasp on my surroundings, nothing felt solid. It felt as if I were falling, forever into an endless void. I could feel myself wanting to scream but nothing came out.

Chapter 7

Was I dead? It was so dark. I saw nothing. I was surrounded by an impenetrable and seemingly endless darkness. The feeling of solid ground beneath my hands awoke my senses. My head ached; the feeling of solid ground was the only thing I could be certain of. It was just so very dark. It was faint but I swore there was a light up ahead. I hoped my mind wasn't playing tricks on me. The more I began to regain my senses the more I was certain that it was a light I had seen. Feeling through the darkness I managed to stand and headed for the only thing I could see, the light. "Ow!" I cursed to the darkness. I had stubbed my toe on something. I bent to the floor and felt around. It was…something, or someone. I felt a face and a hand. The light was right next to me, it was coming from a person. "Who's there?" there was no answer. I didn't need an answer for I knew who it was. "Liz, Liz, wake up, are you alright?" I knew it was Liz. I could feel her tiny face in my hands. The light I had seen had come from her hand; it was a glow-in-the-dark ring. "Adam, Carmen," my calls echoing into the darkness. "Is anyone there?"

"Emma is that you? Where are you? I can't see a thing." It was Adam. I couldn't tell if he was near or far. His voice surrounded me. Startled, I toppled backward off my knees. Liz's ring had grown brighter and brighter. Like a pulse, the glow illuminated the darkness engulfing us. I could just make out Liz's silhouette.

She groaned, "Where am I?" she said, slowly sitting up. From the glow of Liz's ring Adam was able to find his way to us.

"You two alright; where is Carmen?" he asked.

"We're fine, I think," I responded. He helped us to our feet. With Liz leading the way we began to try and figure our way out of this darkness.

Chosen

It was so cold. Through the dim light we were able to distinguish a wall ahead of us. "Looks like this place has an end after all," I stated, placing my palm against the cool stone. I ran my fingers across its bumpy surface when I felt empty air. "Liz over here!" It was a doorway. We hesitated; trying to read each others' expressions in the semi darkness.

"Robert Collier once said, "Playing it safe is probably the most unsafe thing in the world. You cannot stand still. You must go forward," recited Adam. "So, let's find out what lies ahead shall we?" We pressed on into the unknown. Moving forward was just as much of a risk as it would have been to have gone back.

The doorway was the entrance of a tunnel that seemed utterly endless. It felt as if we had been down here for hours, days even. Time ceased to exist, it was merely a concept. There was a light up ahead. A few feet in front of us lights danced across the stone walls. It was the glimmering flames of a torch. I reached for the torch. At least with this we would have more light. But who lit the torch? I questioned. This place was so strange, so surreal. I must be dreaming. With torch in hand we proceeded forward.

"Ahhhhh!" Liz shrieked, tumbling backwards in shock.

We turned, frantic and questioning. Her face had gone paler than usual. Silently she pointed to the wall beside us. There was a face in the rocks. It was a boy. He left the wall and appeared before us in a silvery silhouette. Adam and I stepped back in unison with shock plastered across our faces.

"You shouldn't be here," it spoke.

"Wha... what are you?" I managed to spit out.

"My name is Gonzo. Please don't be frightened. I am an apparition, a spirit. You must come with me; quickly, you should not be here."

Chosen

He was tall, broad shouldered and long hair. He appeared to be completely solid and yet if you looked hard enough you could see right through him. His eyes were what got me. They were not the least bit ghostly. His eyes were a bright turquoise that felt like they could pierce right through me.

"So you're a ghost?" questioned Liz, standing back up.

"Oh, please I hate the term ghost, it sounds so... Casper." He replied.

"Casper?" Adam mouthed at me. I shrugged.

"Hurry, follow me, if they catch you..." He cut off.

"Gonzo, can you tell us where we are?" questioned Liz.

We followed him down the tunnel. "Do you know where our other friend is? Why should we not be here?" I placed my hand on his shoulder, turning him so that he would face me. My hand went right through him. His silvery shoulder turned into nothing but cold icy air. I sucked in my breath, giving a little shiver. He turned to me, piercing me with his gaze.

"There is not a name for this forsaken place, as for your friend, I fear she may be in danger. We must hurry."

The darkness of the tunnel began to diminish as we stepped into a large, bright, round room. The room was filled to the brim with people.

"Who are all these people?" asked Liz.

"These are not people, they are gods," answered Gonzo. "Don't worry they cannot see you."

Adam gave him a questioning look.

He explained. "A long time ago, when the Earth was still young, high above the heavens amongst the stars lay planet Orion, the planet of the gods, known to humans today as Jupiter. Across the known galaxies Orion was the central source of power and a conjugation for every god or goddess that ever existed in history. So it was only fitting that the planet be named after the greatest of them all. A warrior so powerful he ruled over all others, *Orion the Fierce.* He was powerful but more than that he was wise and just. Unfortunately, he was killed in a prodigious battle against a greedy, vindictive, power hungry god not fit to take the thrown. However, winning this battle did not come without a price. The three stars that make up Orion's belt are all that remain of *Orion the Fierce.* Orion's three sons Bishamon, Chokaro, and Fukurokuju equally took their rightful place as heir.

The three sons took the throne as Earth raged into chaos. In order to save the planet from complete annihilation the matter was brought to the three kings of the gods. So in the central city and main hall of Orion, or Jupiter's capital the three brothers Bishamon, Chokaro, and Fukurokuju had called a meeting in order to discuss Earth's current and **growing problem.** This is a recording, gesturing toward the room, a glimmer of the past," explained Gonzo.

"What is this supposed to be a recording *of?*" probed Adam.

"Probably the most important event in history," answered Gonzo.

The three brothers oversaw the crowd at the top of three winding staircases. The oldest, the one named Bishamon stood in the middle. He was short of stature but his presence commanded attention. He wore what appeared to be decorative armor reminiscent of what would be seen on a medieval knight. Everything seemed so surreal. I felt invisible. Gonzo was right, they could not see us.

"What are we going to do?" murmured the crowd.

"Now, now calm down!" his great booming voice full of power and reassurance rumbled through the crowd like thunder during a storm.

A world war had spread across the land creating a blood bath so great Earth was nearly on the brink of extinction. There was a great uprising

Chosen

among the demon tribes creating an imbalance in power. The demons began exploring past the boundaries of their realm and soon got greedy, deciding they would conquer all the known realms, no longer living in hiding.

"We have devised a plan," continued Bishamon. Fukurokuju jerked his head in surprise at his brother. What plan was Bishamon talking about and why had he not bothered to share this information earlier? "We will restore the balance of the two worlds," finished Bishamon. The three brothers left to meet in Bishamon's room.

"Come, you must see," ordered Gonzo. So up we went, ascending the three intricately carved staircases.

I paused staring at the scroll work on the rail, "These are beautiful."

"It is a record of war carved into the stone," informed Gonzo, his expression seeming to harden.

Fukurokuju paced the room fuming with suppressed rage. "How dare you not confer with us first! What makes you think you have the right!" he spat.

"Now Fukuro don't go get your panties in a bunch," Bishamon condescended. Fukurokuju was not only the youngest but the tallest. He was lean with long legs. He had brown hair like his brothers and deep set eyes.

"I have heard Bishamon's plan and it sounds like a secure solution," stated Chokaro.

"You knew? You left me in the dark!" cried Fukurokuju in outrage.

Chokaro had long hair braided down his back and was adorned in a beautifully decorated silk robe. Chokaro was the level headed brother. Quick as a flash Fukurokuju lunged at Bishamon, white with anger he leapt across the room. Bishamon's smug expression disappeared. He grabbed Fukurokuju by the throat and slammed him into the floor. "I suggest you settle down Fukuro," Bishamon snarled. Just then a tap sounded at the door. The brothers looked at one another in unison. With a sigh, Fukurokuju stepped forth to open the door.

Before him, stood a short old man, holding a bowl of breaded shrimp. It was a servant god who went by the name of Hikaro. Hikaro was different than other servant gods. His curiosity usually got the better of him and he was stronger; much more powerful than the average servant god. With a whimsical smile Hikaro held the bowl out to Fukurokuju who proceeded to take the bowl and slammed the door behind him using his foot. With amazing speed and accuracy Hikaro set a marble onto the floor; flicking it into the space between the door and the doorway creating a crack. It was the perfect size for eavesdropping.

Before setting the bowl onto the table Fukurokuju grabbed a handful of the breaded shrimp. So what is this plan?" He questioned through mouthfuls.

"We will handle this quickly and quietly," said Chokaro.

"We are all familiar with the *citizens spell* correct?" continued Bishamon.

"Of course but what does that have to do with saving Earth?" coughed Fukurokuju.

A *citizens spell* was used to create servant gods. "By tweaking the spell we can create warriors in our image to send to Earth's aid," explained Bishamon.

"What is this?" demanded Adam.

"Shush," hissed Gonzo, "just listen." Gonzo's brow furrowed in concentration and confusion. "Something is not right," he said.

Chosen

Without thinking Liz advanced towards him as if to shove him into the wall. She went right through him, crumpling to the floor. An icy chill seeping through her entire body, "Tell us what's going on," she shivered.

"Patience, just listen," he replied. "That servant god is not supposed to be here."

"I suggest we each resign to our own quarters to contemplate the constructions of these replications of our embodiment," proposed Bishamon. "Is that alright with you Fukuro?"

"Yes," he answered. So the brothers left to be alone with their thoughts.

Walking into Fukurokuju's bedroom was like seeing Earth for the first time. It took my breath away. It was a forest, full of creatures I've never even imagined and blanketed by stars. I've always loved the stars. They made me feel small and insignificant, but they are beautiful and full of wonder.

"Shekira," Fukurokuju called out. From the dense forest unearthed a large white stag. "Hey girl, where have you been?" he patted her. "Any ideas?" he said throwing himself into a hammock of vines.

Chapter 8

They met back in Chokaro's room. With a wave of his hand he was able to display every universe that existed. As a process of elimination he chose the one in which they were located. Next, he chose planet Earth. "These warriors will never die. Their bodies may change but their strength will live on. My angel is ready; what say you brothers?" questioned Chokaro.

"Mine is ready." "As is mine," answered the two in unison. Chokaro raised Earth into the center of the room. Chokaro slowly breathed in and out, a green glow illuminated inside of him and came out. "My warrior is named the Jade Magician, he is a warrior of mystical powers and will be a great aid for Earth," he said, shooting the glow into the center of the room, into Earth.

"My turn," said Fukurokuju, repeating the breathy ritual Chokaro had just displayed. "My warrior is an Illusionist; using the power of deception against his opponents," he said, holding a blue glow in front of him he shot it towards Earth.

Bishamon, god of war, stepped up to reveal his angel. A white glow protruded from his chest. "My warrior is simple with no special powers but for a true warrior's heart, strength, a mind set, his only special gift is the gift of extreme balance, Goldenflame," he said shooting the white glow to Earth.

"Now all we have to do is wait," said Chokaro.

"And let things run its course," continued Fukurokuju.

What the three Gods did not know was that just outside their door sat the servant god Hikaro; who had been listening to every word they had spoken. This was a good plan, he thought to himself. These warriors were a

Chosen

part of the gods morphed into beings of incredible power. With all their power however, they had made a mistake. As a team they would be unstoppable, but they would never be able to work together. Their strength and power will only drive them to turn on one another he thought. Despite his status as a simple servant god, Hikaro had a plan. He breathed in and out slowly. A red glow escaped him and as quickly as he could so that the Kings would not see; he shot his glow to Earth. She will be the tie that binds them, he thought to himself, the Komodo Dragon.

"There is a fourth!" exclaimed Gonzo. "I knew it, I could sense it in you," he continued muttering to himself. Suddenly he turned on us. He looked straight at me with those crazy eyes of his. "You are Goldenflame," he stated.

"What?" I questioned, taking a step back.

"That armor that keeps appearing along your skin, it's a part of you. The sudden quickness about you lately; your powers are coming to you," said Gonzo.

"You're insane," said Adam putting himself between me and Gonzo.

"You're the one talking to a ghost," retorted Gonzo. Turning back to me he said, "You wear the shard of two moons; you are Goldenflame."

"Goldenflame is a dude," I said pointing towards the gods.

"Not anymore," he grinned. "And you!" he said pointing at Liz. "You are Illusionist; my guess is that you've conjured things, probably without even realizing it."

The coffee, I thought to myself.

"I don't know what you're talking about, I want out of here," said Liz.

Chosen

"You wear the ring of endless light; there is no doubt about it. You are Illusionist."

"This?" she questioned holding up the hand in which her ring resided. "I got this out of a cereal box!" she shrieked with anger and confusion. She grabbed her ring and threw it to the ground.

"We're out of here," declared Adam, grabbing Liz and me.

"Where are you going to go?" inquired Gonzo, "You don't even know where your friend is."

This struck a chord; quick as lightning Adam turned to face Gonzo. Suppressed anger flashed across his face. The only sign of this was the tightness of his jaw and the fire in his eyes. "Where is she," he growled.

"We better hurry," said Gonzo, turning all corporeal and seeping into the floor. Adam threw himself to the floor as if ready to seep right through it himself. "Ah son of a…"

It was dark. Where am I, where are my friends? Out of the bleak opaque of darkness Carmen managed to spot a small glimmer of light ahead of her. She stood, "Hello? Is anyone there?" her voice echoing into the abyss. When she reached the light she found it to be a ring. "Liz!" she began to scream for she recognized it as hers. Picking up the ring and turning she shrieked in astonishment. A cold ghostly white figure appeared before her.

"Calm down Jade Magician, I am Gonzo; I can take you to your friends. We have to hurry. You shouldn't be here."

Before she could respond she found herself in a large bright room, the light hurting her eyes. She was tackled by someone, she was ready to fight until she realized it was Liz.

Chosen

"Jade Magician, I believe you will need this", said Gonzo, handing her a necklace with a green pendant. "You bear the wrist of roses, you are the Jade Magician. You've been hearing voices, am I right? This will help."

"Goldenflame, this is yours," he handed me...well...it was a stick. What do I need a stick for?

"And you," he looked at Adam. "You are a mistake, but this is yours all the same," he handed Adam a long blade with intricate depictions of what looked to be dragons. "Well now then, you should be on your way."

"But we don't know how to get back, we don't even know where we are," I said.

"Good bye, good luck and don't come back. If you have any questions try the internet, I hear that's all the rage now."

There was a blinding light and a tingling feeling like pins and needles. My vision was blurry but I could make out a dark blob. "What are you doing?" The words blurred together. After they had been repeated several times, I actually understood what was going on. The blob turned into a face and with the face came the words, "What are you doing here?" It was the security guard from earlier. I groaned. My head felt like an anvil. The rest of the gang was just waking up. I pulled on Carmen dragging her to her feet, "Come on, we have to go."

"What are you doing here!" he demanded more loudly, he was starting to get angry. Liz and Adam were on their feet and we were all racing towards the exit. Luckily the security guard was too lazy to bother chasing us.

Chapter 9

It was four in the morning; we had been at the library for hours. No one said anything. We had stopped by the Teen Center for some drinks. The Teen Center was owned and founded by Carmen Jockolva. It had a back room for games, a bar that stretched from one end of the building to the other. It had a stage for karaoke or when Carmen was able to get bands to perform. Liz liked to use the back room as her own personal art studio. The place was empty. It didn't open until 2:00 pm. Liz and Carmen had gone to the back room to unwind. I sat with Adam, sipping my grape soda. I was in desperate need of noise, something to break the silence. The air felt so tense, no one wanted to talk about what had happened, or what didn't happen? Maybe I dreamt it all and I was just being weird. Yeah that's it, we all fell asleep, and I had a weird dream is all.

"Emma?" said Adam.

"Yes?" I said. Adam never got the chance to finish his thought for out came Carmen running and screaming. "Help, help!"

Liz was right behind her, paint brush in hand. "Carmen! Stop, you said you'd pose," she pouted.

"I can't sit still for that long," Carmen answered in defense. In the process of running from Liz she had knocked over several chairs. The sight of them laughing and screaming automatically brightened my mood. Liz and Carmen had entered a paint brush fight, using the brushes as swords. Paint flew everywhere. Liz's paint brush had caught a part of Carmen's green shirt. The red paint against the green made her look like a Christmas tree.

Liz stopped running. "Oh Carmen, I didn't mean to mess up your shirt," she apologized.

Chosen

As if on cue, Carmen clutched the red stain and groaned in agony, twisting to the floor dramatically. "Liz," she whispered, "Come closer, closer, I forgive you my friend I don't think the wound is fatal, my shirt on the other hand, not so much." She continued her death scene, determined to juice all the drama she could into it. "To paint or not to paint! Oh, the agony!"

I busted out laughing. "You're such a premadona." They collapsed into a fit of giggles.

"Who's up for a round of hot chocolate on me?" asked Adam.

"On you? No thanks I'd rather have it in me," said Liz jumping to her feet.

Adam rolled his eyes, "Sarcasm will get you everywhere."

"Says the one being sarcastic," I retorted. He gave me his evil eye but I could see the hint of a smile in his twitchy little lips. All I had to do was flash him my smile and there it was, the grin that lurked behind his attempt to look serious.

"You know I had the weirdest dream when we fell asleep at the library," I said. I waited for a reaction. I got nothing.

"Really, about what?" inquired Adam. He was leaning against the bar very nonchalantly, he had a whip cream mustache from the hot chocolate; I stifled a giggle. Liz was sprawled across one of the tables, content with playing with her hair. Carmen sat on the bar next to me fiddling with her necklace. Her necklace... silver chain, green pendant.

"Um Carmen, where did you get that necklace?"

"Hmm?" she responded, waking from her thoughts. "Oh," she looked down at her necklace as if just realizing it were there. "I don't remember," she replied.

Chosen

"I had a dream about a ghost," said Liz, still playing with her hair. My head jerked up.

"So did I, and you were all there and we were in a big bright room." Adam's jaw tightened, Liz stopped playing with her hair and sat up, and Carmen just sat there in her own thoughts, oblivious. I looked at Adam. "You had the same dream didn't you?"

Silence, I took that as a 'yes'. I grabbed my jacket, "I have to stop by my dad's place. I'll meet up with you later," I waved good bye.

The air outside was dry and windy. The window of Adam's car was cracked open so I reached in to take my skate board. Tarrasa's apartment was only a few blocks down. I had seven brothers luckily Tim and Brad were off to college and Brody was working on finding his own place. I don't think that will go very well though considering he just turned fourteen and didn't have a job. He was hard headed like me. I smiled at the thought, maybe that's why we didn't get along; he was too much like me. My dad flew a plane for a living. You know the ones that have advertisements on the end. He also got paid to give people rides. Tarrasa was an accountant. I know what you're thinking, what could these two people possibly have in common? They met on the internet about three months ago. Tarrasa is a good person. She is kind to my brothers and seems to make my dad happy, but I don't like her. I live in Pleasantville, New Jersey, a misleading name if you ask me, but no one ever asks me. I skidded to a stop. There it was my new home, apartment 34B. I didn't have a key but the door was unlocked so I let myself in.

My two youngest brothers, Joey and Al, rushed at me with hugs. Joey who was four jumped into my arms. "Emmy where have you been!" he whined. I squeezed him tight and bent down to give Al a peck on the cheek.

Chosen

"Sorry I lost track of time," I said. "What are you two doing up so early?" I whispered trying not to wake anyone. I left my jacket, sneakers, and skate board by the door and led the kids to the kitchen.

"We couldn't sleep," replied Al who was six. As the oldest still at home, second to me, Brody slept on the couch so he wouldn't have to share a bed. This was a three bedroom apartment, so Joey and Al shared a bedroom, along with a bed. Zach and Damien were lucky enough to have twin beds but they had to share the closet with Brody. While my dad and Tarrasa shared a room. If I stayed here I would have a sleeping bag in Joey and Al's room. There wasn't much room for my stuff either. I sat Joey and Al on the small counter and opened the refrigerator door. To my luck we had milk.

"Alright, this should help you sleep," I said. I poured two glasses of milk and put it in the microwave to warm it. "So how do you two like the new digs?" I whispered.

"I like it here Emma, will you stay here with us?" asked Joey.

I gave him a smile, "Yes Joey I'll stay here with you." I heard the beep of the microwave telling me the milk was done. I ushered the boys to their room carrying the milk. "Drink up," I said handing it to them. They downed it, hopefully they wouldn't wet the bed, I thought. I tucked the boys back into bed nice and tight. As I was about to leave Al stopped me.

"Emma, will you tell us the story?" he pleaded.

I gave a slight sigh, and then smiled. "Of course." I climbed between the two and they snuggled up next to me waiting for their favorite story. I played with Al's sunflower yellow hair, which always made him sleepy. Joey was in need of a haircut, I made a mental note to cut his hair after school. "Ok, once upon a time there was a brave little bear named Anthony. Anthony was always looking for trouble, excitement, adventure!"

Chosen

Al looked at me with his big brown eyes and I smiled at them. "Adventure," he mumbled back.

"Yes, adventure, little bear Anthony spent all day searching for adventure. Little bear Anthony you must be careful said his mother, you will get hurt and I won't be there to protect you. His mother said this to him every day and everyday Anthony found something dangerous to do. When he fell from a tree his mother caught him. When he was being chased by bees his mother chased the bees away. When he fell down a whole she pulled him out. Little bear Anthony you must be careful she scolded, one day you will get hurt and I won't be there but little bear Anthony new, she would always be there. No matter how many times she scolded or yelled at Anthony, she was always there. On a starry night she tucked little bear Anthony into bed, just like tonight," I smiled. "Little bear Anthony one day you will get hurt and I won't be there. The little bear looked at her and said, 'yes you will mother, for you are a star and stars don't die.' He pointed into the sky and sure enough there she was. She smiled at little bear Anthony. Yes my son I will always be here."

My mother used to tell them this story. It made my heart ache every time I told it. Joey was snoring. "Is she really up there?" asked Al. He was looking out the window at the stars.

"Yes she will always be here," I told him. And I knew he wasn't just talking about the mother bear. At my answer he closed his eyes ready for sleep to over take him.

School started at nine I would have to be ready by eight thirty. It was six o-clock now. I wasn't tired but I didn't want to move, in fear I would wake the boys. Zach, Damien and Brody shared a closet so that means my stuff would be in Joey and Al's closet. Carmen had plenty of room at her house, heck even Adam would take me in though he didn't have much either, but could I really leave the boys? I decided I would stay here for awhile. I wasn't sure how long but I would. At eight o-clock I squeezed out of bed to make breakfast. We had milk, eggs, cinnamon, and bread. So I decided to make French toast, my specialty. I put on some coffee and started making the batter. The smell of coffee woke Brody up.

"When did you get here?" he asked with a big yawn.

"A little after five," I said.

He poured himself some coffee and sat at the counter watching me cook. It wasn't long before I had four done. I put two on a plate and handed it to Brody. "You're an angel," he smiled.

"And you need a brush," I said indicating his hair. "Why don't you wake dad and Tarrasa?" I asked. He finished off the rest of his breakfast before waking the others.

"Good morning sweetheart," said my dad walking in. he hadn't even noticed I was gone. Dad and Tarrasa were soon followed by Zach, Damien, and Al. since Joey wasn't old enough for school I let him sleep in. By the time everyone had finished breakfast Brody was ready for school. He had claimed first shower, lucky. The rest of the morning was hectic with everyone trying to get ready at once. There was only one bathroom in the house; it might as well have been hell. Zach and Damien had taken showers the night before so they were already dressed but they still needed the bathroom to brush their teeth. Tarrasa called second shower and she always took forever. Zach and Damien were twins they were both nine with light brown hair and brown eyes. I imagine that when Al gets older he'll look much like them, accept for his sunflower hair, they'd look like triplets. Joey looked more like me. We both had strawberry blond hair and blue eyes but he had more freckles. I was told I was the spitting image of my mother. Brody was the outcast. He had dark brown hair that could pass for black and blue eyes. In the face he looked just like my father, just in the face. Tarrasa was African American with black curly hair. She was taller than me, about five seven I would have to guess. She had big eye lashes and a killer smile with full lips. She was beautiful. I hated her. I made sure Zach and Damien had all their school supplies. Al's book bag had broken so I patched it together with some duct tape I found. It was almost eight thirty, we should be leaving. Brody had already left; he always walked with his friends. Tarrasa would be taking the younger kids to school. Dad didn't have to work till ten so he would stay with Joey until dropping him off at daycare. Crap, I was going to be late. Everyone was out the door and on their way and I hadn't even had time to shower. I grabbed my clothes out of my closet, took a three minute shower and didn't bother to dry my hair. Racing towards the door I grabbed my book bag and skate board.

  I arrived on campus just as the bell rang. Whew good timing, I thought to myself. I slipped into home room and took my usual seat next to Carmen. Mr. Dick, yes my teacher's name was Mr. Dick, was chattering on about Mendel and pea plants. Carmen glanced at me. "You look like crap," she said. My strawberry blond curls hung down my back, still damp and a bit frizzy. I was 5ft 6in. I wore sneakers, black jeans, a black shirt that said in green letters, 'the zombies are looking for brains, don't worry your safe,' and a grey hoodie. Carmen was 5ft 7in with long dark brown hair. She had flawless skin and frightening green eyes. Today she wore flip flops, blue jeans, and a yellow and white striped tank top. She was a bit larger in the hips than me but she also had bigger boobs so it evened her out.

  "Thanks," I retorted. She handed me a hair tie which I gratefully accepted, pulling my hair into a bun. I hated biology. I find it interesting, it's just the note taking and the listening to someone with the most boring voice on the planet that turns me off. Carmen on the other hand, Ms. Bookworm,

Chosen

loved every subject known to man. She read more than anyone I had ever met. This still surprises me because that girl cannot sit still for her life, but put a book in her face and she shuts off like a light. Sometimes it's as if she has two personalities.

    Homeroom had flown by nicely and second period was almost ending. Ms. Hawthorn had just finished handing out assignments. She was my English teacher, one of the few teachers in the school I actually liked. The bell rang, ah the sweet sound of freedom. It was time for lunch. I headed for one of the picnic tables outside. As usual I hadn't brought lunch. I turned to look behind me and nearly fell off my seat. It was Adam, he had come out of nowhere, freaking ninja, geeze. A moment later Carmen had joined us.

    "Ok I have to talk to you guys and please don't throw me in the loony bin," said Carmen.

    "What's on your mind chica?" I asked.

    She took a breath, "There is voice in my head, that isn't my own, telling me things."

    "Evil things," I teased.

    "It's a she, her name is Lynashia. She says she is a witch; that she died many years ago but that her soul was placed in my necklace so that she could guide new witches. She says her son was the second Jade Magician, or the first reincarnated one. Emma, I had the same dream as you. Am I insane? I want to say that this voice in my head isn't real, but she's hard to ignore."

    Adam lifted the back of his shirt slightly. Between his shoulder blades was a sword with intricate carvings of dragons. "I think that dream was real," said Adam.

    "Hit me," I said.

    "What!" said Adam, taken by surprise.

Chosen

Shrug, "I'll do it," said Carmen reaching over the table. I stopped her, "Slap me hard, not one of those lame taps, hit me like you mean it," I said. She looked at me to see if I was serious. Instead of the smack sound of a hand meeting a cheek, I heard, "Shit! Emma!" hissed Carmen, clutching her hand.

"Lately some sort of armor seems to appear anytime I am in the way of physical harm," I responded.

"And you couldn't have just *said* that?" glared Carmen. "I'm going to need ice, that was mean," she said.

"I have to work after school from five to ten," said Adam.

"I have to pick Joey and Logan up from day care," I said. "I'll meet you at your place?" I asked Carmen. She nodded. "Meet up with us at Carmen's," I told Adam. So that was it. Whatever was going on we would figure this out together.

Fourth period was nearly over. For me this was the longest class of the day. Algebra II, math had never been my strong point. Although Liz was a grade lower than us she was in the same class as me. They had bumped her up to the next class when they discovered her math scores were exceedingly high. I felt a tap on my shoulder. It was Liz, sitting directly behind me. "Pssst Emma," she whispered. Instead of turning around I passed her a note. This teacher hated me enough I didn't need to give her more reasons to dislike me. I didn't want to attract attention to myself so I stretched, yawning. I threw the note at Liz. 'What is it?' was scribbled onto a sheet of torn notebook paper. 'Look, it's the hottie from the video store!' was scribbled on the return note. I looked up. I hadn't noticed any new faces when I walked in. I scanned the room. There was tweedle de and tweedle dumb, jerk wad Johnny, sweet heart Sam, and hey what do you know, there was a new guy and he was really cute. He had the whole tall dark and

Chosen

handsome deal working for him. I turned to Liz and pointed at him. She nodded. So *that* was the guy. As the bell rang I packed up my stuff, ready to leave.

The new guy walked over to Liz. She tried to hide the blush working its way up her cheeks. "Hey," she said. He smiled, wow what a smile, this guy had to have a flaw somewhere.

"You remembered me," he said, looking pleased. He was like a big puppy. I just wanted to eat him up. Instead I walked out of the room.

I turned back to Liz before I left, "Meet you in the parking lot," I said.

"So, ah," he shuffled nervously. "How bout that date?" he asked.

"Sure, when?" she asked.

"Tonight?" he suggested.

"I can't tonight, how about tomorrow?" offered Liz.

"Yeah that would be great," he answered excitedly. "Pick you up at seven?"

"I better just meet you somewhere," answered Liz.

"How do you feel about Chinese food?" inquired Fu.

"Love it," she smiled.

"Great, then how about you meet me at Jin Jins," he said.

Fu walked Liz to the parking lot where they met Carmen and me at her car. "Fu, these are my best friends Carmen and Emma," said Liz, indicating us.

"Hi I'm Fu," he reached out to shake our hands.

"Nice to meet you," I responded.

"I'll see you later Elizabeth," he bent down to kiss her cheek. "I can't wait till Wednesday," Fu smiled and walked away.

"He's cute Liz," said Carmen, climbing into her car.

Chosen

"Let's go, we're going to be late," I said. I had to pick up Joey and Logan from daycare. I had to call my dad and let him know that Joey and Logan would be staying at Carmen's tonight with me and that I would drop them off at daycare tomorrow morning. "Can we stop by my house real quick before heading back to your place?" I asked Carmen. "All my clothes are still there,"

"Sure," she answered.

Chapter 10

After picking up Joey and Logan we stopped by my house. I had grabbed clothes for me and Joey. Logan was a bit smaller than Joey but he could wear his clothes. Carmen pulled into her drive way. The kids loved coming here. For them it was like a palace. We tossed our stuff by the door. I took our clothes to my room. We were at Carmen's house so often that we had claimed our own rooms. Joey would stay in my room and Logan would most likely pick to stay with Carmen. That boy adored Carmen.

So as not to endure Carmen's cooking we ordered pizza. Joey and Logan were content being parked in front of the TV where they would be entranced for hours. The three of us had our noses glued to books. When the boys were tucked in and Adam came over we would talk about the weirdness of the last few days but right now I was more worried about failing algebra. Buzz! It was the doorbell. Yes! This means I can take a break from my homework. Liz answered the door. The pizza guy was some scrawny teenager with a lame uniform and a pizza hat. Liz and I had ordered a pineapple and black olive pizza with cheesy crust. Carmen and the boys were the boring ones that only liked pepperoni.

After dinner we sent the boys to bed. It was 8:00 and Liz had already started yawning. We had finished all our homework so we were content to watch reruns of "Dead like Me." It's dark, cynical, and hilarious. I know we planned on waiting for Adam before talking about what was going on but he wouldn't be here for hours and the boys were asleep. It was the perfect time to talk.

"Liz, I know you had the same dream as we all did. What do you remember?" I asked her. She hadn't been there at lunch today so she wasn't on the same turf as us at the moment.

Chosen

She averted her eyes as she told us, "There was a white boy, a ghost. He told me I had the power of illusion," she laughed. "Crazy, huh."

"We all had that dream," I told her. "I don't think it was a dream. I think it really happened."

She sat up, excited. "I'm not crazy! So what does this mean? Do you think we're really super heroes?" she took a breath.

"Calm down Liz," eased Carmen.

I had Carmen throw something at me to show Liz the armor. It was the only real proof of anything. "I want to try and control when it appears," I told them.

"Look what I can do," said Carmen. "It happened the other night. I don't know if I can do it again. I was angry at the time and it just happened," she crossed her legs Indian style and breathed deeply. She laid her hands on her knees palms open. Two breaths later a spark appeared in her hands. A small flame rested. I tipped over backwards. Water? Fire extinguisher? Did she even have a fire extinguisher? If you hadn't noticed already, I was freaking out.

"Relax Emma, it doesn't hurt and I think I can control it," said Carmen.

"Great, you make fire, Emma has armor. What am I supposed to do?" pouted Liz.

"You made coffee appear," I offered.

"What coffee?" she asked.

"The coffee at Adam's house. He was out of coffee but when you woke up you poured yourself a cup," I informed her.

"Pssh whatever. I didn't make anything magically appear. You're just saying that to make me feel better," she replied.

Chosen

"It's possible," added Carmen. "I mean you are named the Illusionist."

"Hmm," Liz thought. "Hey Carmen why don't you ask your necklace buddy if she knows anything about Illusionist's abilities," asked Liz.

"That's a great idea," I agreed looking to Carmen.

"Lynashia says your power lies in the ability to bend reality. If you believe something to be real then it is real but more importantly others believe. That is all she knows," said Carmen.

"So it's like voodoo?" asked Liz.

"Maybe, try something," said Carmen.

"I don't know, last time I didn't even realize I had done anything," Liz replied, unsure.

"Just try," I encouraged.

She closed her eyes and waved her arms around I could tell she was concentrating; on what I did not know. She opened her eyes looking disappointed. "Nothing happened," she groaned.

"What were you trying to do?" asked Carmen.

"If I tell you I might not be able to do it. I'll try again," she answered. "Close your eyes" she instructed. So we did. "Ok, open them!" she said excitedly. When I opened my eyes Liz was holding a teddy bear.

"Aaww it's so cute!" exclaimed Carmen.

The next couple hours were spent with all of us trying to figure out what we were capable of and how to control it. By the time Adam had gotten off work and had arrived at Carmen's I was able to control the appearance of my armor. Carmen had started floating and Liz was surrounded by strange things that somehow she had created and with an imagination like hers, it was a lot of strange things.

Chosen

"Whoa," was all Adam could muster.

"Here Adam," said Liz holding up a flower she had just created.

"Um thanks?" he said, looking at us for answers.

"We've been practicing these new really cool abilities," said Carmen.

"Adam, we're super heroes!" exclaimed Liz.

There it was, that childlike behavior that only appeared on rare occasions. I had missed it. I liked being reminded of how truly innocent Liz really was. I also admitted to myself that these powers, as freaky as they were, were very…cool. I smiled to myself.

"We don't know what we are," said Adam, bursting our bubbles and tossing Liz's rose to the floor.

I stood up, angry. "Why do you have to be so negative?" I said with vehemence.

"Emma, we don't know what's going on here. Think clearly for a moment will you? What makes you think were supposed to be super heroes? That dream? It was just a dream. I don't have time to be playing pretend. I have enough to worry about," said Adam, sounding annoyed.

"It wasn't a dream and you know it," I told him.

He looked away defeated. Oh yeah, that's right. Who's in charge? I was being smug but at least I kept it to myself. I wanted to know what Adam's newfound ability was. When we were trapped in that book Gonzo had said that Adam was a mistake. Does that mean he doesn't actually have any powers? If that's true, then he gets exactly what he wants out of life. To be normal and he was right, he already had a lot on his plate. He was always stressed out juggling school, a job, and trying to raise his little brother. If he really did have super human abilities, would he use them? Would he have time to use them? And would our morals make us heroes or would having

75

power corrupt us turning us into monsters? I know that I have this gift and if I can I will use it to help people. When I was a kid, my mom was a comic book freak and I always liked the tales of heroes and heroines risking their lives in order to protect people. I never heard of a more noble cause. Was I willing to take up the task? Maybe I was just living a kindergarten fantasy. I had so many unanswered questions. I wanted those answers and I planned on getting them with or without Adam's help.

"Have you noticed anything different about yourself?" asked Carmen. He looked away avoiding the question.

"I think you're faster," said Liz. "Either that or you've gotten quieter cuz you keep sneaking up on me," Liz pointed out. I agreed. He had snuck up on me during lunch earlier.

"Well Lynashia says you have the abilities of a ninja so Liz is probably right," said Carmen. He pulled his dragon sword from where he kept it hidden, between his shoulder blades and set it on the table. I hadn't even noticed he had it on him. He looked so tired.

"Do we get costumes, or disguises to protect our identity?" asked Liz, she was having way too much fun. It didn't seem to bother her a bit; and why should it? We weren't crazy, this was real.

"I don't need a disguise," I told her, making my armor appear.

"Now that's just cheating," she retorted.

"Oh please, you can conjure up anything you want while I get stuck in this," I said pointing to myself. I saw a smile work its way across her cheeks. She did a dramatic twirl and ta da!

"What are you supposed to be? A pirate?" I teased. She frowned. Tattoos swirled their way up her arms. She wore blue gloves that had the fingers cut off, black boots, blue tights, and a black halter top that hung to her knees and clung to her tightly with a blue sash. All that looked fine, it was the bandana she wore that made me bust into a fit of giggles. When I could breathe again I told her.

"Try a mask or anything, just lose the bandana." Carmen groaned.

"What is it?" asked Liz.

"Lyn won't shut up," she frowned. Having a voice in my head other than my own would freak me out. I felt bad for Carmen. "Apparently she's chosen an outfit for me," sighed Carmen.

"Well, let's see it then," demanded Liz.

Carmen snapped her fingers and there it was; she was adorned in a dark green cloak, light green boots, black tights, a light green belt thing, I wasn't sure but it was at her waist, and she had a black top. It didn't cover her shoulders but she had sleeves that went to her wrists. The sleeves were attached to the shirt they just skipped the shoulders.

"I think you look like a slut," I told her.

She glared at me, "I didn't pick it, *she* did," she said in defense.

"I think you look great," said **Adam**.

Carmen ignored him, "I'm wearing a cloak! That is definitely not slutty." She was right. Maybe I was just jealous because they had cool outfits and I got stuck looking like a member of Arthur's round table.

"What about Adam?" I asked.

"What about Adam?" replied Adam.

"Lynashia says to just unsheathe your sword. The getup comes with the territory of being a chosen one." We waited, looking at him. "I am not unsheathing my sword," he told us. Liz stood and stretched. With her yawn came the disappearance of all the weird objects she had conjured.

"I am going to bed, it's late," she told us. She walked over to Adam and kissed his forehead. "You need rest. You're starting to look all wrinkly," she teased.

Chosen

Liz was right, it was late but I wasn't tired. Carmen snapped her fingers bringing back her pj's. She said good night and wished us sweet dreams. On her way upstairs she turned out the lights leaving the TV as our only source of illumination. The TV flickered. I changed it to the music channel where my favorite song 'tik tok' by Kiesha had just started playing.

"You really should get some rest Adam," I told him. He grimaced.

"I know but I can't sleep," he replied.

"Bad dreams?" I questioned. He nodded. I waited hoping he would tell me what they were about without me asking. After a minute had passed by in silence I opened my mouth to ask.

"It's war," he told me. "Fighting, blood, pain, and it's always different, never the same battle." I wasn't sure what to do. It was clear that these dreams were troubling him but I had never been very good at making people feel better. I was about to attempt some consoling words when he spoke some more. "Emma, I think they may be memories from my past lives," he said. That would make sense, I told myself. I sat next to him resting my head on his shoulder. As far as I knew there wasn't a cure for bad dreams.

"I know these dreams bother you but you can't function without sleep. If these really are your past memories maybe you can block them out or I bet you could ask Lynashia if there is a way to get rid of them," I suggested.

"Thank you," he smiled. He grabbed my hand and walked me to my room.

"Promise me you'll sleep," I whispered so as not to wake Joey.

"I promise to try, good night," he whispered back.

78

Chapter 11

In the morning we all got ready for school. I helped to get Joey and Logan ready for daycare. I wore shorts, a tank top, and my purple jacket along with sneakers. I decided to straighten my hair today as a change of pace. I almost always left it curly. Carmen's contacts were bothering her so she switched to glasses. She wore hoop earrings, a red skirt, white blouse, and black boots. Liz as usual wore bracelets that covered her arms, a ring on every finger of her left hand. She wore a black shirt with "Paramore" written across it, dark blue skinny jeans, and flip flops. Adam arrived in the kitchen wearing cargo pants, work boots, and a shirt with a picture of lucky charms on the front. Mornings at Carmen's were always less hectic.

Adam took the boys to daycare while the three of us headed to school.

"The day has just started and my locker is already jammed," sighed Liz.

I did a 180 to make sure no one was looking. I turned my fist into armor and yanked her locker open.

She hugged me. "Thank you!" she said.

Now that my good deed of the day was done I headed to my locker.

Liz threw her book bag into her locker and grabbed her art history book for first period. She slammed her locker shut. Standing on the other side staring at her was Fu.

"Jesus Fu! You sure have a knack for sneaking up on me," she scolded.

"Sorry," he smiled sheepishly. "Here let me take your books for you I'll walk you to class," he told her.

Chosen

She handed him her books and walked off to her class trying to look confident when really her nerves were playing football with her stomach. He was cute, sweet, he was perfect and he liked her!

"I'll see you fourth period?" he asked sounding eager. She tried to hide her blushing, she hated blushing.

"See you fourth period," she answered. They said their goodbyes and he headed off to find his own class.

"Hello ladies," said Johnny popping up next to my locker. I opened so it and slammed it in his face. He groaned holding his nose.

"Sorry," I said stepping over him.

He was so obnoxious. He thinks he is a ladies' man when really he's just a skeeze. If he wasn't the best bartender in town and didn't work at the Teen Center I wouldn't talk to him at all but the fact that I'm there so much gives him the idea that were friends. Johnny was tall, skinny, and black with brown eyes and a buzz cut.

"Whoa hey hold up!" called Johnny as he got to his feet. I sighed, not turning back to wait for him, unfortunately he caught up anyway. "Hey um look I was wondering if you wanted to go to the pep rally with me tonight?"

"No," I told him, trying to push past him and move on.

"Look, I know being with me can be a bit intimidating but you shouldn't let that stop you," he said, blocking my path.

I pushed him. "No Johnny." That skeeze, he can't even look me in the eyes all he does is stare at my breasts and he has the nerve to think I would ever like him. The thought of him made me want to gag.

I took my seat in the back next to Carmen.

Chosen

"I saw you got ambushed by Johnny again. I'm sorry hun. I love how your locker nearly broke his nose though. That was classic," said Carmen with a grin.

School flew by fast today. The next thing I knew it was 4:00pm and the bell was ringing for school to let out. Instead of meeting Fu at the restaurant, Liz rode home with him. Carmen and Adam had already left. I was about a block away from Joey's daycare. One of the wheels of my skateboard was loose. I made a mental note to fix that as I skidded to a stop when the light flashed 'no walking.' The air was dry but there was a slight breeze that made it bearable .When the light flashed 'walk' I was about to skate across when I heard sirens and a loud screeching followed by the sound of crushed metal. An out of control car came tearing from around a corner followed by several police cars. I stepped back onto the curb and held people back to keep them away from the rampaging steal monster. In a man's rush to get back to the safety of the side walk he pushed a little girl who had been standing beside me out of the way. She fell into the street crying. Before I even had time to think, I ran into the street. I wrapped my arms around her, shielding her. I didn't feel it but I knew it had hit me. There was a loud crash followed by an eerie silence. I heard several gasps. When I looked up I was in the middle of the car. I had stopped it dead in the street. The engine looked to be split in two. There were smoke and shattered remnants of the vehicle everywhere. I stood slowly still in my armor. I was hoping no one had seen me without the armor. If there was anything I learned from comic books it was that I needed to keep my identity a secret. I inspected the little girl. She seemed to be fine, just in shock. A woman in the crowd shrieked, "My baby! What have you done to my baby!" I took that as my cue to leave. By the time the police bothered to get out of their cars I was already two blocks away.

Chosen

Now that I was completely out of sight I let my armor vanish. My mind was still processing what had happened. I was a little late picking Joey up but he didn't seem to mind.

"Emma you seem..." he paused, his little face crinkled in concentration as he decided what word to use. "Distracted," he beamed; glad that he could find just the right word.

I laughed, "I just have a lot on my mind Joey," I reassured him. For one I realized I had left my back pack and skateboard at the crime scene. I went back for them once things had settled down. I was also still unsure about what having these powers meant; and what if I had more? Or what if I couldn't control them? What if today I had just been lucky? I rubbed my temple. I was giving myself a headache. When we got back to the house I found Al, doing his homework like a good little boy while Zach and Damien watched TV. The only ones missing were Dad, Tarrasa, and Brody. Brody was probably with his friends.

I searched the cabinets for food and decided on hot dogs for dinner. It was easy and didn't take long to make. "Boys, dinners ready," I announced. They all clambered into the kitchen eager for food. Boys are so gross. My good mood disappeared as soon as Tarrasa arrived home. I cursed myself for already retrieving my book bag and skateboard before making dinner. Now I would have to find a different excuse for getting out of the house. Normally they wouldn't care if I left but Tarrasa wanted 'grown up girl bonding time.' Just the thought of it made me want to gag. Tarrasa walked over to me smiling with those big lips that I hated so much. She had changed from her work clothes into something more comfortable.

"Hey sweetheart," she purred. "How was school?" she moved to brush my hair out of my face but I shifted out of reach.

Chosen

"Fine," I responded. I grabbed a sponge and pretended interest in cleaning the counter. It was obvious that I was trying to ignore her. This caused her to frown but was quickly replaced by a smile. I chuckled to myself. Tarrasa was good at not showing any negative feelings towards me but it was nice to see her illusion slip, even if it were only for a moment.

"Did you learn anything exciting?" she asked.

"Nope," I answered.

She shifted with impatience. This is actually kind of fun I thought to myself. Since she couldn't get anything out of me she started telling me about her day. Ugh never mind, not fun, I corrected myself. Minutes felt like hours. I didn't want to sit here and listen to her boring office humor. She was an accountant! I don't care how hard she tries there is no way to make that job sound fun.

I held up my hand, "I've got to go to the bathroom, Tarrasa, I'll be right back."

The bathroom was too small. I needed air. I was just itching to get out of this small apartment. I opened the window. I closed my eyes and breathed deeply. It was big enough for me to climb out of I noticed. I was on the top floor. If I jumped I wouldn't get hurt thanks to my armor but maybe I could just climb onto the roof instead. I popped the screen out and began to slowly ease myself out. I suppose great balance came with the whole super hero deal. I managed to jump from the window to a flag pole and then onto the roof without a sweat. I sat there hoping no one would find me. The night air was soothing. I couldn't remember the last time I was this relaxed.

"Ouch!" I sat up rubbing my temple. I looked around and saw nothing. I looked up and saw a floating stick. I reached out, stroking it gently. More confidently this time I clasped it and laid it in my lap. It was a golden staff. It appeared to be the same length of my legs, from foot to hip.

Chosen

It's weird. I felt a connection to it somehow like it was an extension of myself. I sat there twisting and twirling it. Where had it come from? It hummed with energy. I soon realized that not only was I able to maneuver it with extreme ease and accuracy but I was indeed connected to it somehow. I could control it with my mind. Without touching it, I had it spin and zoom through the air. I laughed. This was fun.

I woke up the next morning on the roof. I had stayed out all night. My back was stiff from lying against the concrete. I quickly got ready for school. I was almost out the door when I had a crazy idea, but I had always been known to be a little crazy. I climbed back up to the roof and tossed my skateboard to the side. If I really could control this staff maybe with my new found balance I could treat this stick as if it were my skateboard. I took a deep breath, "Here goes nothing," I jumped off the roof and closed my eyes, bracing myself for the feel of my skull hitting concrete but there I was floating in mid air, standing on my stick. I laughed like a crazy person, I probably *was* crazy. I couldn't believe what was happening. I was flying to school. I was a bit wobbly at first but I soon got the hang of it. Even as I landed I couldn't wipe the grin that encompassed my face. I couldn't wait to tell the others.

I ran into Adam on my way to class. "Wow, did you hit the happy pills this morning or what?" he asked.

"I'll tell you at lunch," I beamed. I had never felt such complete freedom. Gravity, my ass.

"Emma!" scolded Carmen. "Stop daydreaming and pay attention." I stuck my tongue out at her. Mr. Dick handed out worksheets and we were to work in pairs. When it came to school Carmen didn't fool around. She loved school. So instead of spilling my guts about how awesome this morning was we sat there and worked on biology. It was a good thing Carmen was in my class. She helped to keep me focused.

When the lunch bell rang I dragged Carmen and Adam behind the building.

"What is it?" asked Carmen.

How should I say this? I looked to make sure we were alone. "This," I smiled. I called the stick and held it in my hand. Before me were two shocked faces. Carmen reached out for it. It shone beneath her fingers.

"Emma?" she questioned.

"I can control it!" I began to tell them all about last night and this morning trying not to leave anything out.

How can they be so calm about this? thought Adam. "No, no, no," he shouted, interrupting our conversation. Startled, I looked at him. He leaned his head against the wall in agony. He looked so angry, but I could see the hidden sadness in him.

"Adam what's your problem? Can't you see we can help people? That we could really make a difference in this god forsaken world!" hissed Carmen, trying not to raise her voice.

"What's wrong with me?" exclaimed Adam. "We are not the embodiments of a god's gift to Earth! We are not saviors! We are not angels! These powers, us, we're killers, nothing more. We were built to kill." What was he hiding behind those dark eyes?

"Adam, you are just a self-centered heartless bastard! You just don't want the responsibility. Here we have a chance to do good and you want to pretend like nothing has happened!" yelled Carmen.

"I *don't* want the responsibility! I don't have time to save people!" he screamed back.

Chosen

The sky grew dark behind the school and a strong spontaneous wind seemed to derive from Carmen. Her necklace glowed in a way that nearly blinded me. I stepped back, a bit frightened. Carmen stood before us…and yet it wasn't Carmen. She certainly looked the same and yet I could sense something oddly different about her. I couldn't quite put my finger on it. Adam placed himself between me and Carmen. So I wasn't imagining things; he could sense it too. "Don't fear me child for I am Lynashia," said Carmen. "Komodo Dragon; you must release your fears of being a killer. I know your dreams frighten you, but you are mistaken, these gifts were placed in your care to help people. You are a chosen one. The reason you have those dreams is because the vessels before you created memories so strong that they have survived years of transport. You see, you were created by a servant god, because of this you do not have the power to block out past memories. Your power does not lie in strength. It is your heart. The Komodo Dragon is about love. It is the Komodo Dragon's heart that enables the Chosen ones to stay together for without it you would all perish. You have the biggest heart of any Komodo Dragon I have ever met and because of that you will be very powerful, but only if you relinquish your fears and trust your heart. You were chosen and you must accept that."

The sky cleared and Carmen collapsed to the ground. We ran to her.

"She's okay," said Adam. He sat her up, she had passed out. "I'm going to take her home.

"Wait she's coming to," I told him.

She tried to talk, it was faint but I still managed to make out what she said. "Not cool, Lyn not cool."

Adam had taken Carmen home to rest. The remainder of the day was spent in a restless stupor. After school I waited for Liz in the parking lot. I told her I'd give her a ride, course she doesn't know that this meant I was going to take her flying. I spotted Liz walking out with Fu. I had walked ahead of them so that they could have time alone together. Their date last night had been a smash. Liz now seemed to have a permanent smile glued to her face.

"Bye Fu!" she waved.

"Emma," she smiled, starry eyed.

Once Fu was out of sight she jumped up and down with enthusiasm. She began to twirl around the parking lot emitting the feeling of bliss. Her arms were wide and she spun like a ballerina on crack. She then ended this display with a fainting motion but instead of landing on hard concrete she fell into the softness of a couch.

"Liz! What are you doing? What if you're seen doing that," I admonished.

"Oh who cares, **no one** is around," she replied lazily, rolling onto her back.

She stood up, "There, it's gone, so stop freaking."

"Wow, you've really gotten a handle on this huh," I said impressed.

She beamed arrogantly. I smiled to myself, "Let me show you what *I* can do."

I was being a hypocrite but no one was around and she had to experience this. I called the staff to me and told Liz to hold on. Before I knew it we were in the air and she was screaming her head off.

It was harder to balance with two people. My eyes watered from the intensity of the wind. I held tight to Liz. At first she was afraid but now she was starting to relax. People had become ants and rooftops were merely specks. I loved this feeling, the feeling of freedom.

"Looks like you have a handle on this too," Liz yelled over the roar of the wind. She held fast to me. I wondered how fast I was capable of

Chosen

going. I'd experiment later but not while Liz was here. It was hard enough holding onto her and maintaining speed as it was. I guessed we were traveling approximately 40mph. Adam had the day off so he had picked up the boys from daycare. We were to meet them at Carmen's place. I still haven't told Liz what happened to Carmen. I hope she is ok. Minutes later we saw it, the Jockolva mansion, my second home. I think my landing was a little too quick because as soon as we touched the ground Liz collapsed and puked. Gross.

    I walked in to find Logan and Joey playing with blocks on the floor. "Hey boys where is Adam?" I asked them.

    "He's upstairs with Carmen," said Joey, greeting me with a smile. I hugged them both.

    "Keep an eye on Aunt Liz for me will you? She's not feeling too great," I explained to them.

    As I was on my way upstairs Adam was coming down. He carried an empty glass in his hand. "She's asleep," he told me. "She's ok, just tired." With that answer I followed him downstairs instead of going to check on Carmen, I didn't want to wake her.

    "She's really mad at Lyn for taking over her body without permission." Adam told me as we sat in the kitchen. I was about to ask how he knew this when he said, "Carmen talks in her sleep."

    "That has to be freaky; having someone take over your body like that," I shuddered at the thought. I couldn't imagine not being able to control my own body.

    "Lyn said she'd get used to it," he grimaced. "I am not looking forward to her visits."

    Adam continued talking but I heard nothing. My mind was far away from this place. I feel so lonely sometimes. I have friends that love me. That should be enough right? I knew that we should talk more about what was happening to the four of us but I'd rather go flying. I need the practice anyway. I couldn't remember ever being as happy as I was when I was flying. I had ridden with my dad in his plane before. He had even let me pilot it myself once. But this feeling was a completely different experience. Even with my newfound power of balance it still took a lot of focus to remain on that stick, add the speed and the danger, the difficulty increases. It was dangerous, it was hard and I loved every minute of it. I headed out the door ready to take flight.

"Stop!" It was Carmen, she was awake and coming down the stairs. "I can't stay long; her body is too weak to contain my power."

"Lyn," I growled. "Get out of her body now or I'll make you."

"You can't keep flying off. Despite your armor you are not invincible. If you fall you will most surely die." She told me, ignoring my earlier threat. With that said she was gone, leaving Carmen to faint yet again.

When she had regained consciousness she looked up at me and started laughing. Had she finally lost it? I wondered.

"Lyn says that through all the centuries of her existence you are the biggest pain."

"Same to her," I grumbled.

Now that I knew Carmen was fine I headed back toward the door when she grabbed my arm. She looked at me, serious now. "Don't go, Lyn knows what she is talking about," said Carmen. I ignored her and left, slamming the door behind me.

"It's like a drug," Adam told Carmen, as he sat down beside her. "She has had a taste and now she is going back for more," he explained.

Chapter 12

At the movie theater Liz found herself enthralled in Fu's words. She was head over heels for this boy. He made her laugh and showered her with gifts and compliments. His soft eyes looked into hers, "You're perfect Elizabeth. I know I haven't known you for very long but now that I have met you I can't imagine my life without you." She stared at him in amazement. Was he for real? Am I really in this movie theater with the hottest guy I've ever met and he likes me? She thought to herself. She could never think straight around him. Maybe this is love? She questioned herself.

After the movie they walked around town for awhile holding hands. The air was cool but Fu kept her warm. The restaurant ahead of them was playing music. Liz didn't know the song but it had one of those beats that just made you want to move. Before she knew it Fu had grabbed her by the hand and dragged her over towards the restaurant. He started dancing next to her. At least she assumed he was dancing. She laughed and joined in however, Liz could actually dance while Fu looked like a fool. "Just the way you are," by Bruno Mars came on once the rhythmic upbeat song they had been dancing to ceased. Liz laughed and was about to continue walking when Fu grabbed her once again. He pulled her into his arms and began to slow dance.

I crashed through the door in a fury. Adam's shocked expression lay before me. I shook with rage and I was going to take it out on him. I grabbed him by the front of his shirt and smacked him into the wall behind him. "Where is he? I know you know! You have connections within the Snakes. That's how you knew they broke into my house. Where is he, Adam?" I screamed at him until my voice ran sore. What really got me was that his expression never changed. He looked at me calmly with his placid eyes waiting for me to cease my rampage.

"Where is he?" I repeated.

"Let me go," he told me. I released him. My anger had been drained out of me. I felt defeated. The only thing left was worry. Adam held me in his arms. Hot tears stung at my eyes but I refused to let them escape. His embrace was warm, I felt safe and secure, it was a feeling I never wanted to lose. Just the feel of his skin against mine calmed my body. "Adam, they took Brody. Why would they do that?" I questioned him.

"I don't know hun but I'm going to find out." He reassured me. He set me down and went to the telephone to make a call. With my anger somewhat subsided my head began to clear. Adam's house was a mess. I suppose he never had time to clean it. In the corner stood Logan. I smiled at the sight of him. "Hey buddy what are you doing?" I called sweetly to him. Was he shaking? "Logan, what's wrong?" He flinched as a reached for him. Oh no, had he been there the whole time? I must have scared him. I went over to him and set him in my lap. He squirmed and cried in my arms but I held to him tightly until he hugged me back. I wiped the tears from his eyes and kissed his forehead. Had I really looked that frightening? "I'm sorry you had to see that," I told him. He nestled his head against my chest. He wasn't afraid anymore, that was good.

Adam walked back into the kitchen with a grim look on his face. "Put him to bed," he told me. It wasn't his bedtime but I did as he asked. Adam had called his neighbor, Peggy to come over and stay with Logan. When they were settled, Adam came back in the kitchen and faced me. Whatever Adam had to say it wasn't good. I began mentally preparing myself for the news. Was Brody ok? I sat at the kitchen table waiting for Adam to speak. "We need to hurry," he told me.

Chosen

I stood up, "Then let's go."

"Emma I'm not precisely sure what is going on but we are going to need Carmen and Liz. The Snakes are stronger somehow. My friend says they are taking orders from a new guy that he has never met before. He says that something strange has happened to the rest of the crew. Scales began to grow along their skin and their eyes have a lizard like appearance to them. He saying they've evolved into something inhuman and it all began when the new head honcho took over. He thinks that the new guy must have drugged them or something. But Emma that's not all, they know who you are. My friend didn't know much, simply that their new leader was looking for someone by the name of Goldenflame."

I sat there too stunned to say anything. This was my fault. I had put Brody in danger but how did this mysterious stranger know who I was and what did he want? Without saying anything I pulled out my cell phone and dialed Carmen's number. I told her to grab Liz and meet us at Adam's house. I let her know that it was urgent and then hung up.

"You know where their hide out is, right?" I asked Adam.

"Yes," he replied.

"Do you know if Brody is ok?" My muscles tensed up as I awaited his answer.

"I don't know Emma," he looked down at the table, unable to look me in the eyes.

I stood up very decisively. "I'm going on ahead. When Carmen and Liz arrive let them know what's going on and meet me there," I told him.

He stood up as well, "I can't let you go there alone."

Carmen hadn't even finished listening to the voice mail I had left her; as soon as she heard Emma's voice she sensed that there was something wrong. She jumped into her car and peeled out of her driveway. She had never heard Emma so anxious, she thought to herself.

Fu was in the middle of telling Liz a funny story about how he had pranked a friend of his when he lived in Brazil; the sound of screeching brakes and the smell of burnt rubber reached them. A red corvette had pulled up alongside of them with the passenger side window rolled down. "Liz, get in we have to go," called Carmen from the vehicle.

"Sorry Fu I have to go," Liz told him as she started to open the door.

"Don't go," he replied. His voice was silky smooth and entranced her, for a moment she hesitated. She wanted to stay with him but she willed herself forward. She opened the door and hopped into the car.

"Sorry Fu," she called back as Carmen sped off.

Adam had convinced me that in order to get my brother back we needed to work as a team. Despite my feelings of urgency I knew he was right. When Carmen and Liz arrived Adam sat them down and explained the situation. When he came to the part about Brody they all looked at me. I turned away. I stood in the corner waiting for Adam to finish. He had told me the location of the Snakes' hide out. I could leave now and have them catch up with me.

"What are we waiting for?" said Liz.

I smiled, that was exactly how I felt. I already had my armor on. My entire body was encompassed in the golden medal except for my head. I twirled the staff between my fingers out of impatience. In a heartbeat they were all ready. Carmen snapped her fingers and her green cloak appeared. Liz conjured up her outfit. Tattoos worked their way up her arms and she

Chosen

wore a black halter top, blue tights, black boots, and most importantly a mask. Adam had unsheathed his sword. His outfit automatically appeared. He was adorned in black with red marks around the collar and red boots. A black mask covered his face. "Lyn says this is the first she has seen this disguise on a Komodo Dragon because all your past lives were Kunoichi," said Carmen.

"What does that mean?" asked Liz.

"Kunoichi means female ninja," replied Adam. "All my past lives were women," Liz stifled a laugh. "And all of yours were men," he told her.

"Odd," I thought to myself. How the gender roles seemed totally reversed.

We ran to the warehouse where Adam said the Snakes were using it as a chop shop for stolen cars and drug deals. We left the car at Adam's in fear that they would trace the license plate. Good thing we were all in good physical condition because the warehouse was a good fifteen miles away. We flew most of the way there. We found that all of us could fly except Adam so I carried him on my staff. I wasn't sure what kind of trouble we would encounter nor the severity of danger. All I know is that I have to protect my brother. If it wasn't for me he wouldn't even be in this mess. I needed to know who took him and how they found out who I was. Was it creepy hobo? Is he still after my powers? How could I be so careless by assuming that he was a thing of the past? I'd almost forgotten about him. I'm coming Brody, hold on. A few more blocks to go and we would be there. My heart tightened in my chest. I had to keep a clear head. This wasn't a high school street fight. We were going up against drug dealers and car thieves. Not to mention Adam had said that they would be stronger than normal humans. I didn't know what I was headed towards all I knew was that I had to go. I took solace in the knowledge that my friends had my back but I also did not want to put them in harms' way.

"Stop," said Adam. We stood before a deserted warehouse.

"Ugh, it smells awful," said Liz.

"Why would their hide out be this dump?" asked Carmen.

"That is exactly why," responded Adam. Screams began to emerge from within the worn down building.

"Brody," I flew to the roof and crashed through the window. I didn't have time for stealth. Glass was strewn everywhere. I found myself surrounded by giant lizard men. I didn't know any other way to describe the sight of these monstrous creatures. The warehouse was three stories high and filled to the brim with lizard men. I didn't see a single human in the joint there was a slight semblance of the humans they once were. Each man was engulfed in red scales. Their eyes were cold and reptilian. Some had tails and some did not. I could tell by their clothes which ones were female and which were male. It grossed me out when the creatures began slithering their tongues at me.

With staff in hand I took a fighting stance. I managed to fend the first ten off with ease. A circle of unconscious bodies surrounded me; along with a seemingly endless hoard behind them. I jumped into the air and with my newfound balancing ability and sprinted across the ceiling beams. The sound of more screams hurt my heart. It was coming from the room next door. A ruckus could be heard on the floor below me. It must be the others, I thought. I kicked down the door. The room was empty save for a chain that ran from the ceiling and hung to the center of the room. Just high enough to lift Brody off his feet. He dangled back and forth. His arms were stretched over his head and the chains cut him at the wrists. His shirt was bloody with cuts. With a dazed look in his eyes he rolled his head to look at me. Oh God,

Chosen

he looked so young. Beside him was a table full of various torture devices. I tensed up. The room was dark but I felt the presence of someone else in the room. From the corner of my eye I saw the flicker of a shadow. Lunging forward I caught him in my grasp. I held before me a scrawny little snake demon. I made my voice sound deep so that Brody wouldn't recognize me, "Did you do this?" I questioned it. It shook with fear and began to cry.

"Yes, yes I did but please don't hurt me I was only following orders." I slit his throat without a second thought.

"I saw that," said Adam coming up behind me. "I told you these powers would corrupt us, you killed that poor creature as it begged for mercy." He looked away, disgusted.

"Poor creature!" I shouted, indignant. "That *poor* creature did that to an innocent boy!" I pointed my staff towards Brody.

"You didn't kill him because you thought it was the right thing. You did it out of cold revenge. Well revenge can't reverse what has happened to Brody. You are filled with pain and guilt but don't let that effect you the next time we are forced into battle! Got it?" His words burned me for there was fire in his voice. I clenched my fists.

"How dare you talk to me about *feelings*. You are a cold emotionless bastard and always have been!" I was glad I had my helmet on so that he couldn't see my face. I held Brody in my arms. He shook under my touch but when he realized I had come to help him, not harm him, he fell into my arms. He pasted out from exhaustion.

I turned to Adam, "How many left outside?"

"None," replied Carmen finally finding us. "Unfortunately the mastermind behind this got away; Liz ran after him but she lost him."

"Which way did he go? I'll go after him myself," I told her. "I need to catch him or my family may never be safe."

Chosen

"Forget it," said Carmen. "Adam, take your sword and place it on Brody," she told him. Adam did as he was told.

"Why am I doing this?" he asked.

I lay Brody down while Adam placed the sword against his chest. The sword glowed and Brody groaned in agony. "You're hurting him," I vexed. I pushed the dragon blade away from Brody but his chest was completely empty of all the cuts that had once been there.

"Now all we have to do is erase his memory," said Carmen.

"Wait, are you sure you can do that without making any mistakes?" I asked her.

"Don't worry I've been doing this for centuries," she winked at me. She placed her palm over his forehead.

"Thank you, all of you," I looked at my three friends.

"What now?" asked Liz. "We have a slew of either dead or unconscious lizard dudes out there. Do we just leave them?"

"Yes," said Carmen. "They are demons now and will be taken care of by the spirit police. You gotta admit Lyn's vast knowledge comes in handy," she smiled.

I have never really been one for hugs but I hugged all of them. "I have to take Brody home now," I told them.

Chapter 13

A few days after the incident we found ourselves hanging out at the Teen Center. Adam hadn't said anything about the other night. I took that as a sign that he had forgiven me for my harsh words. Brody was okay and didn't remember a thing. A song had come on that Liz liked so she pulled Adam to his feet and they began to dance. Liz was born an artist and dancing was just another art form for her to conquer. Her body moved like liquid, rhythmic and graceful. I laughed at the sight of Adam trying to keep up with her. Carmen and I shared a look of understanding and smiled at one another. She pulled out her phone and recorded the show.

"This is going on my status," she told me. I laughed so hard I began to cry. That was until Liz grabbed my hand and pulled me to my feet. Ah crap, I thought to myself. I probably looked just as bad as Adam.

"Quit hiding behind that camera and come join us," I yelled at Carmen. I took her hands in mine and twirled her around. It looked so gay that we erupted into a fit of giggles. Our amusement had caught the attention of the rest of the club which only increased our maddening laughter. It took us a few minutes to regain our composure.

"Hey Johnny, another round of drinks for my girls," requested Adam. Adam and I had our usual water, Liz ordered grape soda and Carmen had orange juice with a touch of vodka.

Liz looked at her at Carmen. "Since when do you drink?" she asked with a puzzled expression.

"Don't judge me," she told us, "you have no idea what a headache Lyn can be."

The door to the Teen Center opened, letting in the afternoon light. "Whoa," said Liz. I turned my head in the direction she was looking. The woman who had walked in the door was beautiful. She had long blond hair that ran like waves down her spine. Her face was a display of delicate features, save for fierce sapphire eyes and when she smiled she lit up the room. She walked up to the bar and began talking to Johnny. "She's very pretty," commented Liz. "Yet there is something off about her." She struggled to find the words, "something … fake."

"Her boobs," said Adam. "No woman's boobs could look that perfect."

"Oh they are real I assure you," said the woman, walking towards us. She heard him from all away across the room? Adam's eyes widened and his face had turned a deep shade of red. Adam was blushing! Adam never blushes!

"Hi my name is Ulrica, I am looking for Carmen Jockolva," she smiled at us.

"That's me," said Carmen, standing up. "How may I help you?" They shook hands.

"I was wondering if you had any job openings here at the Teen Center," she asked. Carmen thought for a moment.

"Well we could use an extra DJ if you're up for it," she told Ulrica.

"Really? That would be fantastic!" Ulrica beamed with excitement.

"When can you start?"

"I could start right now if you like," she replied.

Carmen laughed at her enthusiasm, "Tonight eight-o-clock and be on time," she told the girl.

"Ugh, Adam, have some self control. You were practically drooling over her and couldn't keep your eyes off her ass," I scolded.

What a pervert, I thought to myself. I left the Teen Center and took to the air. The nerve of that guy. Whatever, it's not like I even care. The

99

Chosen

wind had picked up making it harder for me to keep my balance and it sure got cold being so high up. I swung by my dad's office and snatched his flight goggles and jacket. I was getting better and better at flying every day. I smiled and released the security of my staff beneath my feet. I let myself free fall. The air rushing past my ears was so loud that it seemed silent. I could do this for hours, I thought to myself. Instead I braced myself and got ready to stop the free fall. I folded my arms across my chest and closed my legs. This caused my body to spin out of control. I called the staff to me. When I felt its strength against my feet I used it to slow me down until I was able to stand on it steadily. I took a deep breath. I had lost track of time, the sun had begun to set. I should be heading home. On my way back it started to rain.

When I got home I took a quick shower before heading to the Teen Center. I promised Carmen I'd help stock some shelves. She was paying me but I would have done it anyway. I may not be the nicest person but I am loyal. Most of the school was afraid of me due to a few street fights but that was a long time ago. Apparently when people say, "Don't worry it's in the past," they really mean, "I'm only being nice so you don't hurt me, psycho." I don't mind it though. I like being left alone. There was already a long line waiting to get into the Teen Center. I went in through the back and was greeted with warmth and noise. The place is really busy tonight, I thought to myself. I worked my way through the crowd to find the rest of the gang. Ulrica was doing a good job for her first night. The place was off the wall.

"Hey Emma," welcomed Liz.

I slid into the booth next to Carmen and Adam. They were engrossed in a conversation about our powers and recent apparition activity. Adam was pulling information out of Carmen. She still wasn't strong enough to handle Lynashia's power but the witch was still trapped inside Carmen treating her as if she were merely a messenger. Liz ignored the both of them and used Carmen's cell phone to txt her boyfriend.

"Tell me about our past lives," Adam told Carmen.

"There are some things she cannot reveal," replied Carmen. Carmen made a face as if Lynashia had said something she didn't want to hear.

"What is it?" I asked her.

"Lyn keeps complaining about how weak we are."

"But maybe we wouldn't be so weak if she would tell us more about our powers," said Adam.

"Emma, you have to stop being so reckless. If you are knocked unconscious your armor will disappear and won't be able to protect you. At the warehouse the other night you not only put yourself in danger but the whole team. If you ever pull a stunt like that again I will personally teach you the meaning of pain. Adam," she turned to him. "Lyn has never seen a greater Komodo Dragon than you, yet you deny your gift. Stop running like a coward and face it. I sense a strange great aura overlooking the city, yet Liz sees nothing. As the Illusionist she has the power to see behind deception and magical barriers and should be aware of this. " She looked at Liz when she said this. Liz looked up from the cell phone; she hadn't been paying attention so she was clueless to Carmen's stare.

"Leave her alone she's just a kid," I defended her.

"She is not just a kid, she is a powerful super being." Carmen retorted.

"How much of this is Lynashia speaking and how much is your own opinion?" inquired Adam.

"The facts about your powers are Lyn, the rest is me," she replied.

This information gave me a lot to think about. It made me want to get stronger. I wanted to surpass my ancestors in power.

Chosen

"We just got these powers. Why does she expect so much so soon?" I asked Carmen.

"Because she is worried," said Carmen.

"About what?" asked Adam.

"I don't know," said Carmen. She seemed deep in thought. The simple fact that Lynashia was worried probably gave her goose bumps.

'Pretty Rave Girl' by *I am x-ray* stole my attention from the table. I smiled at Carmen and she got up to join me on the dance floor. Time to lighten up the mood around here. We were soon followed by a couple of guys. My heart was pounding. I was up to my ears in adrenaline. The guy placed his hands on my hips and we began to move as one. I looked at Carmen and we screamed the lyrics together. I loved this song.

As it ended "Ulrica out," was on the loud speaker. It must be her break; time for Greg to take over. I squirmed through the crowd heading to the bathroom. I splashed some water on my face to cool down. As I was exiting the restroom I bumped into Ulrica. She was taller than me, more slender, and just downright prettier. Normally things like that didn't bother me but for some reason I found myself jealous of Ulrica. What was worse is that I found that I liked her. She seemed genuinely nice and was unaware of her good looks. I could see why Adam liked her.

"Hi," she said.

"Hey, you're doing a great job for your first night," I told her, trying to be polite.

"Really? Thanks," this compliment seemed to please her. "Hey wanna maybe hang out sometime, get a bite to eat or something?" she asked me. Before I could answer the ground shook beneath me. I stumbled from the sudden movement. The shelves along the hallway began to fall and even parts of the ceiling crumbled. I felt a sharp pain to the back of my head.

My head felt like an anvil. I tried opening my eyes but it only made it worse. I was disoriented and my vision blurred but I forced myself to focus on my surroundings. I was lying on the floor. Someone was on top of me. It was Ulrica. She was hurt as well. Broken glass and a shelf pinned her against me. Her body shielded me from the glass. Had Ulrica saved my life? I tried to move but couldn't.

Ulrica lifted her head, "Good, you're alive," she told me. I tried to respond but found that I was unable to speak. "You hit your head pretty bad," she continued. She tried giving me a reassuring smile but it turned into a grimace. She was in pain. The shelf, that would have pierced my heart while I was unconscious, drove into her shoulder blade. Blood ran down her back from where the glass had cut her skin. "There was an earthquake," explained Ulrica. Ulrica had been closer to the doorway, why hadn't she gone to safety? Ulrica was hurt because of me. I had to help her but I was so dizzy I wasn't even sure if I could. I tried to move my arm but Ulrica stopped me. "Don't over exert yourself, help will come," she said sternly.

"You are hurt. I have to get this thing off of you," I protested, my voice was weak but I was glad to find that I was able to speak. I called my staff to me and used it to pry the shelf off of Ulrica. Ulrica's head was towards me so she never noticed the staff. Unfortunately moving the shelf also provoked her wounded shoulder. It must have been painful but she didn't say a word. She stuck out her chin and bore the pain. My vision blurred again but Ulrica held me tight against her; hauling me to safety.

Chapter 14

My eyes opened to bright lights. I was in a white room and an I.V. was stuck in my arm. I looked around. I was also hooked up to a heart monitor and there was a bandage on my head. To the left of me sat Adam and in the chair behind him was Ulrica; fast asleep. "Adam," I said. At the sound of my voice he rushed to my side.

"Emma, what took you so long?" he smiled at me with relief.

"Why didn't you just heal me?" I asked. He pointed to Ulrica.

"She hasn't left your side I didn't want to reveal our powers to her," answered Adam.

"Help me get these things off of me," I pulled out the I.V. and disconnected the heart monitor.

"Geez you are stubborn," he pulled out his sword and laid the sheath on my head healing my injury. With the wires off of me the heart monitor flat lined. This got the attention of several nurses and Ulrica.

"Ma'am you need to lie down. Please get back in bed," ordered one of the nurses. Ugh they were irritating.

Adam whispered in my ear, "Pretend to still be a little hurt so you seem normal."

"You know you're cute when you're sleeping," Ulrica said, coming beside my bed to look at me.

"I'm glad you're ok," I told her.

I looked at Adam, "How is everyone else? Is the Teen Center still intact?" "How is your shoulder? I asked Ulrica.

"All good. I heal quickly," she winked at me. Healed? How long was I out?

Chosen

"Carmen and Liz are outside talking to Gonzo. You and Ulrica seem to be the only ones who sustained any real damage. The Teen Center is a mess but it's nothing we can't fix," said Adam. "Ulrica, you have been great but can the four of us speak to Emma alone for a minute?" he asked her.

As Ulrica stepped out Carmen, Liz and Gonzo walked in. Liz and Carmen greeted me with discharged worry while Gonzo appeared to be all business. "What is going on? Why are you here?" I looked at Gonzo. He looked human, no longer see through.

"That earthquake was an omen," he responded. "Something dark has entered New Jersey and that earthquake was its way of making itself known. I fear you may be faced with many more challenges similar to the Snake Demons. I came here to warn you. Lesser demons are somehow managing to enter into your world. The Reciliux is trying to sort out the cause but they have no leads. As chosen angels of Earth you must do your duty and defeat this dark creature," said Gonzo.

"Reciliux?" asked Liz.

"They are an ancient order dedicated to the protection of Earth from outside forces," answered Carmen.

By now Gonzo had left and Carmen was working on getting me discharged. I let Gonzo's warning sink in. What were we supposed to do?

Liz sat on the edge of my bed playing with the buttons on the remote making the bed move up and down. "Guess what," said Liz.

"What?" I replied.

"Ulrica is a werewolf," she said bluntly. I looked at her like she was crazy. She sighed and turned to me, "Remember when I said there was something fake about her? Well I see it now; she has wolf ears, a tail, and even claws."

Chosen

For some reason I wasn't surprised. Maybe I had just gotten used to my life getting stranger and stranger. "She's not bad though right? I mean she saved my life," I asked Liz.

She shrugged, "How should I know? I can see through her disguise not her soul. If you really want to know, how about you go on that date she asked you on," suggested Liz.

Date? Oh right Ulrica wanted to hang out. "It is not a date," I corrected her.

"Well you better make that clear to Ulrica. I think she has a crush on you. Poor Adam was crushed when he found out she was a lesbian," said Liz.

I sighed. My life was getting too complicated. "Does Ulrica know who we are or that we know she is a werewolf?" I asked Liz. Liz shook her head. Should I tell her? I wondered. "If she is a demon she might have a clue as to what is going on with the other demons," I told Liz.

"That is exactly why I want you to go hang out with her. Find out as much as you can," said Carmen, walking in.

"You are free. Let's go," said Adam, following after Carmen.

The following weekend, Ulrica had taken me to see a movie that had just come our in theaters. At first I thought it was lame. It was about a middle aged woman who lived a sorry excuse for a life. I understood that it was meant to be funny but I merely found her pathetic. Later I admitted that there were a few scenes that left me giggling. This didn't feel like a date. I was beginning to think that Liz was wrong about Ulrica. Yes she picked me up and yes she paid for my movie ticket but friends do that too. Carmen has treated Liz and me to a movie. Carmen and Adam are the only ones with cars so they usually drive when we hang out. I've paid for Liz before. We all tend to take care of each other without a second thought. How was I supposed to know if she was gay? It's not like she had a flashing sign above her head and she certainly didn't act manly. Weren't lesbians supposed to be butch? I decided it didn't matter. I liked Ulrica. I wanted to be her friend and if she did like me more than that I would simply let her know she wasn't my type. What worried me was her being a werewolf. She may have saved my life but what if that was a trick to gain my trust?

"Hey look," Ulrica pointed to an ice cream cart. "Want anything?" she asked.

"Oh, no thank you I'm not hungry," I told her. My stomach growled in protest and I frowned at it.

"Two vanilla cones please," ordered Ulrica to the ice cream vendor. She handed me one. "I don't have a problem paying Emma." I gave her a sheepish grin.

"I just don't like being taken care of. You have already saved my life I should be the one buying you ice cream," I told her. She shrugged it off as if I was being ridiculous. We sat at a bench in the park listening to a band playing across the street. We were having fun but I was still suspicious.

Carmen's voice echoed in my memory, "Find out what you can, but be careful she could be dangerous." I had yet to bring up the supernatural. If Liz was wrong…I stopped myself. I had faith in Liz and her abilities. Ulrica was smiling talking about the bands' music and how they were obviously influenced by Fats Domino; one of the first rock musicians from the 50's. "Ulrica, do you believe in the supernatural?"

She looked at me and laughed, "Yeah, I guess so, why?"

I took a deep breath, "I know you are a werewolf," I blurted. She stared at me and I blushed; feeling embarrassed.

Chosen

I am Emma Carter. I have faced Snake demons, been sucked into a book, and frequently free fall through the skies with no fear. I am stubborn and proud. Yet Ulrica had just made me blush. She had made Adam blush as well. Was that a werewolf power?

"Does that question mean that you are the infamous Illusionist?" she responded. Our friendly day had taken a serious turn.

"No, I am Goldenflame," I admitted cautiously.

She smiled, "Yes I see it; you are the warrior, not the trickster. Yes, I am a werewolf, does that frighten you?" asked Ulrica. There was a twinkle of amusement in her eyes and she was smiling but I didn't see any of that. I saw only loneliness. As if this question had always yielded poor results.

"You came to the Teen Center looking for the Chosen Angels didn't you? How did you know where to find us and why? Are you a good demon or do you mean us harm?" I questioned her.

Her enchanting eyes looked upon me as if I were a naive child. "Your magical aura is so strong any lower level demon could sense it. You four haven't learned to mask your aura yet. Why hasn't lady Lynashia taught you this? I came in search of you because of the dark presence that now surrounds this city. This is my home and I aim to protect it." said Ulrica. As an afterthought she added, "By the way I am not a demon, I am a werewolf. Calling me a demon is a huge insult." Her words appeared to be sincere.

"How do you know so much about us?" I wondered.

"My dear I am much older than I look," she left me with that.

It was my turn to smile at her. "Well I hope I can live up to your expectations as Goldenflame."

"So, we're friends then?" she looked at me hopefully.

"Yes, Ulrica we are friends," I told her. Ulrica's ears perked up. I wished I could see past her glamour to see her little doggy ears.

"Do you smell that?" she asked me.

"What?" I asked confused.

From the lake across the street emerged a six legged creature with horns. It was the size of two cars piled on top of one another. I stood up, "What is that thing?"

"It is a Bukavac demon. They live in basically any type of body of water but why on Earth would it reveal itself in the daylight," wondered Ulrica. "Call your friends, we could handle it on our own but you need the team work practice."

I did as she instructed; screams and the sound of people clamoring to get away from the monster erupted throughout the park. "Carmen we have a demon problem at the park across from Egg Harbor," I called her. Carmen's voice on the other end of the phone was a little muffled.

"How bad is it?" she asked. "You are going to have to hold your own or call Liz. Adam and I are also dealing with a creature that seems to be hungry for humans and spits out acid," her voice sounded distant and I could hear the sound of objects being smashed or crushed. "But hey my aim has improved," she said excitedly. "I gotta go hun be careful with your demon. We'll head over as soon as we are done," she told me.

I had called Liz next and she said she was on her way. "We are on our own," I told Ulrica, quickly transforming into Goldenflame.

"Call me Wolvina," she told me as her glamour faded away, revealing her dog ears, a tail and claws. Her outfit changed into a silver furred mini skirt and a fur top, which could have been mistaken for a bra.

"Are you really going to fight in that?" I asked.

"When you are part wolf, clothes seem pointless. In fact, I fight better naked," she winked at me and dove at the Bukavac demon.

Chosen

I managed to break two of its legs before it had a chance to strike back. Wolvina had used her sharp claws to tear through its rough skin. The demon charged me but I jumped straight into the air to land on its back. Even with my Goldenflame gifted balance I found it difficult to remain on the creature's backside. It thrashed and twisted with irregular movements. Wolvina was beside me. She dug her claws into its back to keep herself up.

"We have to end this before it destroys anything else," she yelled at me.

I stabbed it through the head and it instantly collapsed to the ground. Wolvina had lost her balance so I jumped off of the misshapen beast to pull her away from Bukavac's falling body. Green puss oozed out from where Wolvina and I had torn through it. "I guess we are even now," said Wolvina.

"Looks like I'm late," said Liz, rushing to my side. She was dressed as Illusionist. "Sorry I'm late I got held up. Whoa, that thing is ugly, what is it?" Liz pointed in the direction of what used to be the Bukavac demon, her face a canvas of unconcealed repugnance.

"Were you attacked by a demon also?" I asked her.

"No a bank robbery; get it "held up," she laughed at her own joke.

"Trickster," greeted Ulrica. "Ulri...I mean Wolvina," responded Liz.

"Wait how did you know her name was Wolvina?" I asked Liz, confused.

Liz seemed taken aback, "Um I don't know," she scratched her head in wonder.

Then we heard a laugh from Ulrica. "Your past life hated me. Knowing my name just means your soul remembers me," she grinned at Liz, obviously finding it amusing. If Ulrica knew our past lives she really must be old.

"We have to find Jade Magician and Komodo Dragon. They are fighting a demon," I told her.

"Don't worry about that, Jade Magician blew it up," said Adam striding towards us. He bent down to whisper in Liz's ear, "You sure she's gay?" Liz shrugged. Adam's eyes had popped out at the sight of Ulrica in wolf form.

We spent the rest of the day training. Not only honing our individual skills but our ability to work as one. Carmen had me practice hitting things with my staff and my balance. Adam's defensive attacks were nearly perfect so he was practicing offense. Liz's conjuring abilities were incredible but for the moment she wasn't working on perfecting her powers but building up her physical strength. Carmen had also informed her that she needed to meditate.

Carmen was talking Gonzo once again to see if he had any leads for us. So far every demon sighting appeared to be random. According to Gonzo the fighting would only get worse from here on out. I was hoping Carmen had a plan. Gonzo disappeared and Carmen walked out onto the abandoned air field we were using as a training ground. She looked worried and determined, "From now on I want every piece of free time you have used for training."

Many days have passed since then. Those days turned to weeks. The passage of time felt nonexistent. We got used to fearing for our lives. The intensity and rush of a battle became second nature. Two months had overtaken us; turning us into something far exceeding human expectations. Winter had entered New Jersey and with it, snow. It was a cold night. The

Chosen

wind blew hard enough to make me wear my dad's flight jacket while I was out. I came in through the top story window of Carmen's mansion. The terrace I stood on overlooked the ballroom. Adam and Carmen sat together at the grand piano playing something from Mozart. They had been friends since childhood so playing together was effortless. They were so in tuned with one another that the result was beautiful. I could tell something was wrong with Adam though. Not in his physical appearance or expression but merely in the way he played. I could feel something *off* about him. I decided to follow him home and make sure he was ok. They continued to play for another half hour. I didn't make my presence known. I was content to sit and listen. When they were finished Adam gave Carmen a peck on the forehead and said his goodbyes. Soon after I found myself knocking on the door to his house. He answered it wearing only a pair of sweat pants. The sight of his naked chest brought heat to my cheeks. I hoped he didn't notice. As usual his hair was a mess and he looked worn out but he managed to give me a smile anyway. He stepped aside to let me in. He walked to the couch, sat down, and buried his head in his hands.

"What's wrong Adam?" I probed. There was no reply. I started petting his head; something my mom used to do when I was upset.

"You are going to make me fall asleep if you keep that up," said Adam breaking the silence.

"Sorry," I laughed at him. "Is it the nightmares again? You seem different, I can't explain it," I told him.

"What you are sensing is probably the mixture of relief and fear," he replied. "Tonight is my last night with Logan. I am placing him in the care of my neighbor, Peg. She is moving to Texas come tomorrow. Also, I am moving in with Carmen." He explained further.

Chosen

I took a minute before saying anything, "I think you are doing the right thing." He looked up startled. Obviously he wasn't expecting that sort of response.

"You are just saying that to make me feel better," he grumbled.

"Now Adam, when have you ever known me to not be upfront with you. You know I don't sugar coat anything. If I thought you were being selfish or stupid I would tell you. In fact I think you are doing the best thing for Logan. Texas is far away but considering what has been going down lately far away is a good thing. Plus, you can barely manage school and work so you hardly ever have time to be with him. I know it hurts you to send him away but you are providing him a chance at a better future than this hell hole," I said. "Don't worry, he is never going to forget his big brother, his hero."

He just stared at me until finally I told him to stop being a creep. "Thank you for coming over Emma."

"Yeah, well I didn't have anything better to do," I told him. I started to get up to leave when he grabbed my hand.

"Will you stay with me tonight?" he asked, not looking at me. "In case I have a nightmare," he explained.

I was hesitant at first. I don't know why, it's not like we haven't slept in the same house before but this was different, this was just the two of us, no Carmen or Liz. "Um yeah, sure Adam I'll stay," I sat back down. He laid his head in my lap and was asleep in an instant.

Chapter 15

We packed ourselves into Carmen's tiny car and headed towards the docks. Carmen decided that amongst all the fighting and training we all deserved a break so she was taking us to hang out on one of her yachts. She even invited Ulrica and her friend Dane. Dane was also a werewolf and was second in command of their pack.

"Ulrica is with a guy, she must be straight," said Adam triumphantly.

"Your chances with her haven't changed, it looks like she's taken," said Liz, squashing his hopes in an instant.

Ulrica was wearing a little black dress while Dane looked unworthy of her by sporting simple jeans, a t-shirt, and a brown leather jacket.

"What are *they* doing here?" asked Liz. She pointed towards **Derik** and **Johnny**.

"Johnny overheard me talking about the party, as for Derik I have no idea," answered Carmen. Carmen went to get something to drink. Adam went to talk to Ulrica and Liz found Fu. I sighed I guess I should go talk to Derik.

"Why are you here?" I asked him.

"You haven't been returning my calls," he told me. He **stood there** wearing his same stupid football jacket as always. He looked angry but desperate all at once.

"Yeah, I was hoping you would get the hint and leave me alone," I retorted.

"Emma please listen to me, **I love you and** I want to be with you," he pleaded.

"Damn it, Derik! I am tired of your lies; you cheated on me! You do not cheat on people you are in love with."

"Emm," he tried to talk but I stopped him.

"Leave now," I ordered and he did as told, though he made a show of sulking his way back down to the docks. I leaned against the rails of the ship and watched him leave. A sense of accomplishment overtook me.

"Good job," said Johnny coming up behind me and handing me a drink. He had been watching the whole show. The drink he had given me was lemonade, my favorite. I drank it quickly and made Johnny get me another.

"Derik is kind of a player when it comes to women. You deserve better than that," said Johnny.

"Your one to talk," I mumbled in return.

He smiled at me, "Hey, I can't help it if the ladies find me irresistible." He was trying his best to be his version of charming and failing miserably.

I rolled my eyes at him in response. I didn't want to be here with him. Tonight was supposed to celebrate how far the Chosen Angels had come and yet somehow it had turned into a big thing. Word had somehow gotten out that Carmen was throwing a party. People from school and the Teen Center started showing up and the music got louder with every song. The rest of Ulrica's pack and various other supernatural friends we had made in the last few weeks managed to arrive. Adam had befriended a ninja clan and after stopping a forest fire we were welcomed by a few fairies. They weren't itty bitty like Tinkerbell. They were average height and though they had wings, normal humans were not able to see them.

Chosen

"So what is the deal with this Fu guy?" asked Johnny. He had been talking to me for a while now but I hadn't been paying attention. He didn't seem to have noticed.

"What about him?" I answered. "He is Liz's boyfriend."

I guess I just find it strange. Liz has always been so spunky but when he is around she's as docile as a kitten and she does everything he asks without question. It just isn't *her*.

"I wanna know how he does it," Johnny was looking at Fu with admiration and it disgusted me but Johnny was right.

I had noticed a difference in Liz, little subtle changes but sometimes it's the little things that make all the difference. She had been skipping the last few training sessions and talked to Carmen and me less and less every day. It was like she was somehow being pulled away from us. Now that everyone lived with Carmen it should have been much easier getting the group together but I only half lived there and Liz was constantly ditching us for Fu.

"She is mean to me now, it really hurts my feelings," said Johnny.

"Liz has always hated you," I said absent mindedly. Then he looked at me seriously for a minute.

"Not like this," he set down his drink and walked away leaving me alone on the crowded ship.

Johnny was a disgusting pervert so why should I take anything he says to heart? I shouldn't but the fact that even *he* noticed something off about Liz began to worry me. I went to find Carmen. She hated parties. She must be throwing a fit trying to figure out why so many people were here. I was right; I found her freaking out at the ships chef because there wasn't enough food.

116

Chosen

"Listen these people were not planned but I am not about to kick them all out so if we don't have food then run and get pizza," she told a scrawny looking man and handed him a wad of cash.

"Oh Emma!" she shouted with relief when she saw me. I gave her a hug to try and calm her down.

"Maybe if there is no food they will all leave?" this thought made her laugh.

Carmen had always been a very hospitable person; then again she could always afford to be. Her brown hair was strewn across her face from the night's wind. She let me baby her into a sense of calm. Her striking green eyes looked down at me behind box like glasses.

"You hug me any tighter and your boobs will suffocate me," I complained.

She giggled and let go. "You are just jealous," she turned around and smacked her butt in my direction, "Of my amazing assets."

"I know I am," said Adam. I punched him.

"Don't worry Emma, you may not be as filled out but you certainly have the face of an angel," he wrapped his arms around me in an embrace but I shrugged him off.

"What did Derik want?" he asked me.

"He wants me back," I told him.

"You said no right?" probed Adam.

"Maybe," I turned away from him.

"Emma, you can't really be taking him back! He doesn't care about you!" Adam was furious.

"What does it matter to you!" I turned around to face him. We were nose to nose screaming at each other. I could feel his warm breath against my cheek. "Why don't you go back to Ulrica and leave me alone!"

"Fine I will!" fuming he stormed off.

"What is the matter with you two?" asked Carmen stunned.

"Nothing," I replied a bit too quickly.

"Are you really getting back with Derik?" Carmen asked me.

I looked at her like she was crazy, "Of course not."

"Then why would you let Adam think that you were?" I didn't have an answer for her. Something about Adam always made me act irrational, I couldn't explain it. It wasn't like Adam actually cared or anything. He was just nosey I told myself.

A goblin came up to us. He looked like a normal human boy but he was glamoured just like Ulrica and the fairies were. We had met him after fighting off a group of dark ninjas attempting to destroy his home but I could not remember his name. He bowed to Carmen. "Tank you for tis wonderful party Jade Magician but I gots some news tat teres a fire downtown tat the humans can't seem to put out. Something about water not putting it out. I don't tink the humans can handle tis on tere own so I wanted to tell you," He bowed again then left us to join his friends.

"Think we should all go?" I asked Carmen.

"Yeah I'll grab Adam, you go get Liz," she told me but before she went to get Adam I stopped her.

"How are we supposed to stop a fire that water won't put out?"

"We will figure it out when we get there," and she left.

Liz was on the other side of the ship so I weaved my way through the crowd. I sighed knowing that I could fly above all these people's heads in a heartbeat if I wanted to. Soon enough I was able to find Liz, she was with Fu.

Chosen

"Liz we gotta go something has come up," I told her. She knew I was talking business because "something came up," was our decided code line for when the Chosen Angels were needed.

Before Liz could say good bye to Fu he stopped her. "Stay with me," his silky voice whispered in her ear.

"Let's go," I repeated.

I saw her expression change and when she looked at me I saw a Liz that I had never seen before. I didn't know how to describe it but what I saw was not the Liz I knew.

"I'm staying here with Fu. Whatever it is I'm sure you guys can handle it," she told me.

I was shocked, "Why?" I asked her.

"I love him," she looked up at him adoringly, "I can't imagine ever leaving his side again," she said to put it simply.

I felt a piece of me die inside. Liz was my best friend. To think that she didn't care tore me apart but I left without a word and hoped that she couldn't see through my stoic mask.

I could feel the heat of the flames as I neared downtown Pleasantville. "We have managed to evacuate most of the cities occupants but the fire department refuses to leave," said Adam, as I pulled up beside him riding my staff.

"Idiots, if they can't put it out why do they bother staying? They should just leave it to us before they get hurt," I replied.

"They stay because they are brave men, not idiots," corrected Carmen.

"Where is Liz?" asked Adam.

Chosen

"She's not coming; why are the flames green?" I asked hoping to divert the conversation back to the problem rather than Liz. I knew Carmen was going to ask so I stopped her before she had a chance, "We will deal with Liz after we put out this fire, any ideas?" I stared at the raging fire below us watching the green inferno dance as if it were alive.

"We have to hurry before the whole city turns to ash," said Adam.

We both looked at Carmen hopefully. "Why do I always have to make the plan!" she complained.

"Because you're kind of the unofficial leader," I scorned.

She sighed, "This fire isn't natural. I think perhaps it is being controlled by someone or something. I suggest we split up and search for whoever is manipulating the fire," said Carmen. With those orders we split up scouring the city and trying not to get burned.

Adam and Carmen searched the outskirts of the city assuming that the one responsible would be somewhere watching nearby but I dove straight for the heart of the city. Something told me to go to the center and there I would find the source of this disaster. Unfortunately my armor only seemed to make things worse and increased the heat of the flames. If Liz were here maybe she could…no I couldn't think about her right now, I told myself. I gripped my staff in both hands and swung it so hard that I managed to part the flames. I ran through as fast as I could knowing that they would return just as quickly as I had put them out. By repeating this act several times I managed to make it to the center unscathed. A few feet from me sitting cross legged was a man. He looked to be meditating. I hid behind a wall so he wouldn't notice me. Carmen was right these flames were being controlled so all I had to do was stop him. The man looked human, he was black with white lines under his eyes wearing red pants and shoes and completely engulfed in green flames. I couldn't help but stare at him. He looked to be in

120

his early twenties, his chin was stern and his body appeared to be all muscle. A frontal assault wouldn't work. There was no way I could make it through those flames in time to get near him. Carmen was the brains, all I knew was how to fight; strategy had never been my thing. I rubbed my forehead in irritation. The only thing I could think of is if I could somehow distract him. I scanned the ground for something to throw. Surrounding my feet were a few crumpled bricks amongst other debris, "This will do nicely," I thought to myself. . Hopefully I could finish this quickly. The smoke was making it impossible to breath and the heat of the flames was making me weak. Spinning my staff I cleared a path to the meditating man and hurled several bricks in his direction.

    I fist pumped the air, elated that my plan had worked. He was distracted. I had nailed him right in the face! The fire turned red and orange so he was no longer in control! But my joy soon turned to fear. The man had seen me and was headed my way. I felt swallowed by a new assault of green flames. One of the bricks I had thrown had broken his nose. By pissing him off, I seemed to only have made things worse. He ran towards me with fury in his eyes. He screamed at me in a language I didn't understand. I was trapped in his flames.

    "Stop it!" I screamed. My heart was pounding he would reach me in seconds and I couldn't move. "What do I do, what do I do," my mind raced. With a round house kick, the man crushed my torso and I fell to the ground crippled. He continued to scream out in a language I couldn't recognize. I was free of his flames but his kicks were relentless.

    "Speak English you monster!" I spit back through clenched teeth.

    "You filthy protector of vermin. You don't even deserve to be in my presence. By siding with the humans you are no better than they are," said the man.

Chosen

    Controlling my staff with my mind I swung him into the nearest building so hard that his body left an indentation. Unfortunately that wouldn't slow him down for long but it bought me enough time to struggle to my feet and hide. My pace was slow and painful but I made my way towards a crumpled down building. My armor had disappeared. I no longer had enough strength to make it stay. Leaning against a wall I slid to the ground to rest. I closed my eyes praying that he wouldn't find me.

    The green flames raged like an envious animal trapped in a cage and set lose upon its prey. Inside the city I watched as my surroundings burned, turning to a crisp ashy death. The smoke entered my lungs. I gasped for air but only received more of the hideous fumes. However, there was still life left in that forsaken blaze. To my surprise and dismay I heard the cries of a young child. I hoped my ears deceived me but I knew better. Trapped in a nearby apartment was a little girl. I was just able to make out her face at a broken window. The fire had not yet reached her. If I attempted to reach her I would be disregarding my last and only protection I had left against the man of flames.

    "Damn kid," I grumbled. In agony, I hobbled to the broken window. "Stop crying and give me your hand," I ordered. I pulled her small body out of the window cutting my arm in the process but the little girl was ok at least. I wiped the tears from her dirty face and inspected her but found no injuries. "Let's get you out of here," I said taking her hand.

    "Who are you?" her small voice replied.

    I smiled at her, "Just your friendly neighborhood super hero."

    "Filthy insect, did you really think you could hide from me?" That voice.

Chosen

I stood frozen, I wasn't strong enough to fight him nor was I strong enough to run. My only instinct was to protect the child. Using my body as a shield I prepared myself for the impact of another kick but it never came. I turned around, wondering why the man hadn't hit me. Adam stood in front of me holding the man's foot in his hand. He had arrived just in time. My heart lifted. I had never been so happy to see him. "Touch her again and I'll have your head!" he seethed. With ninja speed and accuracy Adam had pinned the man to the ground his hand clenching his neck. The man writhed helplessly. He could not defend himself against Adam's iron fist.

Carmen was by my side. I went limp in her arms; relief washing over me. "Hang in there," she told me. The little girl had stopped crying watching us. Her family came running up to claim her and Carmen told them to take her to safety.

The man began to cry out his indiscernible dialect but switched to English when Adam tightened his grip. "Make the flames go out," demanded Adam.

"Can't," the man breathed.

"Why not," asked Adam.

"Orders," said the man.

Adam's grip was so tight the man could hardly get any words out. "From who?" questioned Carmen.

"God of Wi," the man gasped.

"Komodo loosen your grip," said Carmen. Adam did as he was told.

"All hail the God of Wind," said the man.

"Hail this," said Adam, knocking him unconscious.

"The Reciliux will take him into custody and interrogate him," said Carmen. With the man unconscious the flames went out instantly.

Chosen

Adam placed his sword on my body and my wounds began to disappear. He took my hand, "You need to be more careful," Was that worry in his face? My heart beat a little faster.

I stood up, "Took you long enough to get here," I retorted.

Chapter 16

Our wait for the Reciliux to arrive wasn't long. The man was dragged underground to a secret bunker to be questioned. The Reciliux's methods were harsh and he would most likely not survive but we had our own questions that needed answers so we followed after them into the shadows of the Reciliux.

Carmen beckoned to one of the guards watching over the unconscious man, "I want to speak with Gonzo."

The guard bowed before Carmen, "Master Gonzo is away on other matters. In his stead is Master Tio," she replied.

"You will inform us the moment he wakes. We want to interrogate the prisoner as well," Carmen told the guard.

"For someone who hates politics and doesn't wish to inherit her family's company you make a pretty good leader," I told her, "You are so bossy," I picked on her.

Carmen replied by sticking her tongue out at me. Just as we were all about to lose our patience we heard a storm of feet approaching from the left corridor. At least ten bodies headed towards us. In the lead was a female with blue scaly skin and small white horns protruding from her forehead.

"You must be Tio," addressed Carmen.

"It's Master Tio, but yes," the fierce woman replied in a surprisingly high pitched voice. "Is our guest still sleeping?" Tio asked the guard.

"Yes," she replied.

Tio smirked, "Then let's wake him up shall we?" she nodded at us to enter the interrogation chamber. "I have to warn you that this room

Chosen

prevents anyone from using their powers, that includes you three," she informed us after we entered.

"Way to give a heads up," Adam muttered under his breath.

The man sat in a metal chair in the middle of the room. He was strapped to it by his wrists, ankles, and neck. We watched as Tio slapped him continuously until the man awoke. "Who do you work for!" demanded Tio.

"You can't make me talk," the man answered.

"He said he was sent by the God of Wind," said Adam.

Tio stopped her slapping and turned to Adam, "The God of Wind?" Adam nodded. Tio rolled her eyes, "He is lying, the God of Wind is dead, has been for centuries," she told us.

The man looked at Tio, "You are a demon and yet you continue to serve humans? You are a disgrace to our race. You will die with them."

"Is that a threat?" she slapped him.

"Who do you work for?" Adam questioned him.

"I work toward the destruction of your infernal species. I work for the superiority of demon kind and I work for the one who promises us salvation!" he screamed.

"So the one claiming to be the God of Wind wants to destroy all humans and open the demon portal?" asked Tio.

"All hail the God of Wind," the man began to laugh psychotically.

"Maybe he's finally lost it?" I suggested.

"One…two…three. Three angels," the man looked from one of us to the other. "Where is the fourth I wonder?" he started to laugh some more.

My insides went cold and I shared a glance with Carmen. We had left Liz by herself unguarded!

Chosen

"You cannot defeat the God of Wind. You should join our cause while you still can," the man instructed Tio.

"Tough talk for one strapped to a chair," she slapped him.

"What have you done with Illusionist!" I demanded, slamming my fist into the table. The man broke into a wide grin, "Your fourth Angel is gone," he shook his head, "Tsk tsk, perhaps you should have taken better care of your loved ones. You wouldn't want another mishap with your brother now would you?" I was about to lunge at him when Adam grabbed me around the waist and pulled me out of the room, followed by Carmen. "Your Illusionist is dead!" he yelled after us.

"Master Tio, inform us of any new information as soon as possible," Carmen ordered as we were leaving the room.

Tears stung my eyes but I pushed them back, "This is all my fault," I told them. "When I left to fight the fire all I could think about was how Liz was abandoning us. It never occurred to me that I had left her alone," I hung my head in shame. I had failed Liz. As we ran out of the underground bunker to the surface all I could think about was the day we had first met. I could see it as clear as day. It was only a year ago that I had befriended Liz. At the time, I was just fifteen and she was fourteen. She had been sitting at a park bench crying. I had seen her for at least an hour before deciding to go over to her. When I sat down she hadn't even noticed me but eventually I got her to stop crying. That day I promised to protect her. I promised that Adam, Carmen, and I would be her family and I meant every word. She was my younger sister and I had left her without thinking of the consequences. For all I knew she could be hurt somewhere…or worse. "Your Illusionist is dead!" echoed in my subconscious.

Adam grabbed my hand, "This isn't your fault. He is probably lying anyway. I'm sure she is fine," he tried to reassure me. I hoped he was right.

Chosen

When we finally made it back to the yacht the party had ended. Only Ulrica and Dane remained; Liz was nowhere to be found. Ulrica and Dane looked upset and wouldn't look us in the eyes.

"What's wrong? Have you seen Liz?" I asked in urgency.

"After you all left something happened," said Dane, his voice had a thick Australian accent. Finally he managed to look us in the eyes, "A sea creature took Liz underwater. We were unable to locate the body. Ow," Ulrica had punched his arm.

Her," she corrected him.

"Right we were unable to find her body," Dane told us.

"And what are you doing now! Just standing here! We have to look for her!" I glared at them.

Ulrica grabbed my arm, "The smell of blood is thick," she still couldn't look at me. Was the boat spinning? I felt so dizzy. I started to shake but Ulrica held to me fast. "I'm so sorry Emma," there was sorrow in her voice.

I pushed her away, "You're wrong." I felt sick. Adam and Carmen's faces were wet with tears they let them fall freely not caring who saw and not bothering to wipe them away. We looked pathetic. The three most powerful heroes mankind has ever seen were sobbing uncontrollably.

"They are unfit for battle what are we supposed to do?" I overheard Dane ask Ulrica.

"We fight no matter what; they can stay here," she informed him.

A wave of nausea had left me and I stood up, "Wait, what battle?" I asked her. She looked unwilling to tell me. I wiped my face, "I lost it for a minute but it won't happen again," I was determined. Adam and Carmen had recovered too. The yacht was a mess of debris. When we had landed I assumed it was from the party but now looking closer I saw the remnants of a fight. "Were there any other casualties?" I asked them.

"No," said Dane.

"Tell us about this battle you are so worried about," ordered Carmen, her attitude was harsher than ever.

"Just before you arrived Gonzo sent us a message," began Ulrica. "Gonzo has been receiving intelligence for months from a spy working with someone claiming to be the God of Wind."

"Gonzo has known about this for months!" interrupted Adam.

"Yes, and his spy has informed us that the God of Wind has been reorganizing the demon community and looks to be planning an invasion," continued Dane.

"How big of an invasion?" asked Carmen. I was afraid to find out.

"He has an army the size of New Jersey. The good news is we know where and when he plans to strike," said Ulrica.

"And that is?" asked Adam.

"Two days from now," answered Ulrica.

"Two days! Two days! How are we supposed to be prepared to take on an army in two days? That is not enough time," Adam was freaking out and I didn't blame him.

"Gonzo has already sent this message to all of the Reciliux," said Dane.

"Two days is not enough time but it's not impossible," reassured Carmen. "We have Ulrica's pack along with two others; we have the ninja clan, and the witches' coven, not to mention the Reciliux. These are all very powerful fighters and if the God of Wind underestimates us we will have that on our side," said Carmen.

"You really believe we can do this?" I asked her.

Chosen

She looked at me, "I believe we have to try."

The next two days were spent in a flurry of activity. All delegations were made and strategies proposed. It was hard to believe how quickly word had spread and how many were willing to fight on our side. As long as all this hard work could be kept under wraps then we may be able to put the God of Wind on the offensive but I didn't want to get my hopes up. The Chosen Angels had been put in charge of one thousand soldiers while Tio, Gonzo, Ulrica, and several other factions would lead others to attack the God of Wind from various directions. With this battle, the God of Wind would be rearing his ugly head and making himself vulnerable. He would no longer be able to hide from us. We had ten hours before the invasion. The enemy's plan was to create a small portal so that they could rapidly take over Atlantic City. They planned to use the ocean as a boundary and head inland; because of this we stationed troops underwater to attack them from behind. The Chosen Angel's troops were to attack from below, with them as a distraction we would attack from above. Adam and I were to keep the demons at bay while Carmen and five other witches attempted to close the portal. It was a good plan, if we could reach the portal in time. I couldn't sit still. The intensity of this battle weighed on everyone's mind and in a few minutes we were to be placed at our designated stations.

I saw Ulrica, she was too far for me to hear what she was saying but she looked to be giving a last minute speech to her pack. Ulrica and her pack's usual fighting apparel was mere fur but for a battle such as this they had upgraded to, well it was still fur but more of it. They had completely transformed into wolves, except for Ulrica who kept her human form. When she was done talking I waved her over. I wanted to wish her good luck and to be safe. I smiled when she got close enough to hear me, "Hey Ulrica," She looked at the ground as if considering something when she looked up she looked more sure of herself. Was she mad at me? I wondered. She pushed me against the wall and just as I was about to fight back she kissed me. I was so stunned I couldn't move. She took my hand and placed it against her heart which pounded like a hammer beneath my touch. Her sapphire eyes urged me to listen. "I have lived a very long time but my heart has never beat this fast for anyone," she let go and turned to join her pack who were already heading out, not even giving me a chance to respond. My face was still flushed. What the hell had just happened?

"That was hot," said Adam coming up beside me.

"Perve," I scoffed.

Adam placed his hand in mine. It gave me comfort; in return I squeezed it tightly. With Adam by my side I could conquer the world. With him I was safe. I held onto those feelings as we were about to head out with the other soldiers. Carmen joined us and the three of us stood together knowing that we were merely prolonging the inevitable.

"We have to try," I told them.

"For them," continued Carmen, indicating the buildings below us.

It was hard to believe that only a few months earlier our biggest concern was getting our homework in on time. My voice lowered to a whisper. Saying these words so softly as if to stop time itself, remembering that moment and those words forever, "Angels, time to fly."